Edwin Hubbell Chapin

The Crown of Thorns

A Token for the Sorrowing

Edwin Hubbell Chapin

The Crown of Thorns
A Token for the Sorrowing

ISBN/EAN: 9783337267230

Printed in Europe, USA, Canada, Australia, Japan

Cover: Foto ©Andreas Hilbeck / pixelio.de

More available books at **www.hansebooks.com**

THE

CROWN OF THORNS.

 A Token

FOR

THE SORROWING.

BY

E. H. CHAPIN.

BOSTON:
PUBLISHED BY A. TOMPKINS,
38 & 40 CORNHILL.
1860.

PREFACE.

ONE of the discourses in this volume — "The Mission of Little Children" — was written just after the death of a dear son, and was published in pamphlet form. The edition having become exhausted sooner than the demand, it was deemed advisable to reprint it; and accordingly it is now presented to the reader, accompanied by others of a similar cast, most of them growing out of the same experience. This fact will account for any repetition of sentiment which may appear in these discourses, especially as they were written without any reference to one another.

To the sorrowing, then, this little volume is tendered, with the author's sympathy and affection. Upon its pages he has poured out some of the sentiments of his own heartfelt experience, knowing that they will find a response in theirs, and hoping that the book may do a work of consolation and of healing. If it impresses upon any the general sentiment which it contains, — the sentiment of religious resignation and triumph in affliction; if it shall cause any tearful vision to take the Christian view of sorrow; if it shall teach any troubled soul to endure and hope; if it shall lead any weary spirit to the Fountain of consolation; in one word, if it shall help any, by Christ's strength, to weave the thorns that wound them into a crown, I shall be richly rewarded, and, I trust, grateful to that God to whose service I dedicate this book, invoking his blessing upon it.

E. H. C.

May, 1860.

CONTENTS.

The Three Tabernacles.

The Three Tabernacles.

And Peter answered and said to Jesus, Master, it is good for us to be here : and let us make three tabernacles ; one for thee, and one for Moses, and one for Elias. MARK ix. 5.

CAUGHT up in glory and in rapture, the Apostle seems to have forgotten the world from which he had ascended, and to which he still belonged, and to have craved permanent shelter and extatic communion within the mystic splendors that brightened the Mount of Transfiguration. But it was true, not only as to the confusion of his faculties, but the purport of his desire, that "he knew not what he said." For even "while he yet spake," the cloud overshadowed them, the heavenly forms vanished, they found themselves with Jesus alone, and an awful

Voice summoned them from contemplation to duty, — from vision to work.

Peter knew not what he said. He would have converted the means into an end. He and his fellow-disciples had been called to follow Christ not that they might see visions, but had been permitted to see visions that they might follow Christ. Just previous to that celestial interview, Jesus had announced to them his own painful doom, and had swept away their conceit of Messianic glories involved with earthly pomp and dominion, by his declaration of the self-denial, the shame, and the suffering which lay in the path of those who really espoused his cause and entered into his kingdom. They needed such a revelation as this, then, upon the Mount of Transfiguration, to support them under the stroke which had shaken their earthly delusion, and let in glimpses of the sadder truth. It was well that they should behold the leaders of the old dispensation confirming and ministering to the greatness of the new, and the religion which was to go down into the dark places of the earth made manifest in its authority and its source from Heaven. It was well that they should see their Master glorified, that they might be strengthened to see him crucified. It was well that Moses and Elias stood at the font, when they were about to be baptized into their apostleship of suffering, and labor, and helping finish the work which these glorious elders helped begin. But that great work still lay before them, and to rest here would be to stop upon the threshold; — to have kept the vision would have thwarted the purpose. Upon a far higher summit, and at a far distant time — with fields of toil and tracts of blood between — would that which was meant as an inspiration for their souls become fixed for their sight, and tabernacles that should never perish enclose a glory that should never pass away.

You may have anticipated the lessons for ourselves which I propose to draw from this unconsidered request of Peter. At least, you will readily perceive that it *does* contain suggestions applicable to our daily life. For I proceed, at once, to ask you if it is not a fact that *often we would like to remain where, and to have what, is not best for us?* Do not illustrations of this simple thought occur easily to your minds? Does not man often desire, as it were, to build his tabernacles here or there, when due consideration, and after-experience will convince him that it was not the place to abide; that it was better that the good he craved, or the class of relations to which he clung, should not be permanent? In order to give effect to this train of reflection, let me direct you to some specific instances in which this desire is manifested.

Perhaps I may say, without any over-refinement upon my topic, that there are three things in life to which the desires of men especially cling, — three tabernacles which upon the slope of this world they would like to build. I speak now, it is to be remembered, of desires of impulse, not of deliberation, — of desires often felt, if not expressed. And I say, in the first place, that there are certain *conditions in life itself* that it sometimes appears desirable to retain. Sometimes, from the heart of a man, there breaks forth a sigh for perpetual *youth*. In the perplexities of mature years, — in the experience of selfishness, and hollowness, and bitter disappointment; in the surfeit of pleasure; in utter weariness of the world, — he exclaims, "O! give me back that sweet morning of my days, when all my feelings were fresh, and the heart was wet with a perpetual dew. Give me the untried strength; the undeceived trust; the credulous imagination, that bathed all things in molten glory, and filled the unknown world with infinite possibilities." Sad with scepticism, and tired with speculation, he cries out for that faith that needed no other confirmation than the tones of a mother's voice, and found God everywhere in the soft pressure of her love; and when his steps begin to hesitate, and he finds himself among the long shadows, and the frailty and fear of the body overcome the prophecies of the soul, and no religious assurance lights and lifts up his mind, how he wishes for some fountain of restoration that shall bring back his bloom and his strengh, and make him always young! "Why have such experiences as decline, and decay, and death?" he asks. "Is it not good for us to be ever young? Why should not the body be a tabernacle of constant youth, and life be always thus fresh, and buoyant, and innocent, and confiding? Or, if we must, at last, die, why all this sad experience, — this incoming of weakness, — this slipping away of life and power?"

But this is a feeling which no wise or good man ever cherishes long. For he knows that the richest experiences, and the best achievements of life, come *after* the period of youth; spring out of this very sadness, and suffering, and rough struggle in the world, which an unthinking sentimentality deplores. Ah, my friends, in spite of our trials, our weariness, our sad knowledge of men and things; in spite of the declining years among which so many of us are standing, and the tokens of decay that are coming upon us; nay, in spite even of our very sins; who would go back to the hours of his youthful experience, and have the shadow stand still at that point · upon the dial of his life? Who, for the sake of its innocence and its freshness, would empty the treasury of his broader knowledge, and surrender the strength that he has gathered in effort and endurance? Who, for its careless joy, would exchange the heart-warm friendships that have been annealed in the vicissitudes of years, — the love that sheds a richer light upon our path, as its vista lengthens, or has drawn our thoughts into the glory that is beyond the vail? Nay, even if his being has been most frivolous and aimless, or vile, — in the penitent throb with which this is felt to be so, there is a spring of

active power which exists not in the dreams of
the youth; and the sense of guilt and of misery
is the stirring of a life infinitely deeper than that
early flow of vitality and consciousness which
sparkles as it runs.   Build a tabernacle for perpetual youth, and say "It is good to be here"?
It cannot be so; and it is well that it cannot.
Our post is not the Mount of Vision, but the
Field of Labor; and we can find no rest in Eden
until we have passed through Gethsemane.

Equally vain is the desire for some condition
in life which shall be free from care, and want,
and the burden of toil.   I suppose most people
do, at times, wish for such a lot, and secretly
or openly repine at the terms upon which they
are compelled to live.   The deepest fancy in the
heart of the most busy men is repose — retire-
ment — command of time and means, untram-
meled by any imperative claim.   And yet who is
there that, thrown into such a position, would
find it for his real welfare, and would be truly

happy? Perhaps the most restless being in the
world is the man who need do nothing but keep
still. The old soldier fights all his battles over
again, and the retired merchant spreads the sails
of his thought upon new ventures, or comes un-
easily down to snuff the air of traffic, and feel
the jar of wheels. I suppose there is nobody
whose condition is so deplorable, so ghastly, as
his whose lot many may be disposed to envy,
— a man at the top of this world's ease, —
crammed to repletion with what is called "enjoyment;" ministered to by every luxury, — the
entire surface of his life so smooth with completeness that there is not a jut to hang a hope on, —
so obsequiously gratified in every specific want
that he feels miserable from the very lack of
wanting. As in such a case there can be no
religious life — which never permits us to rest
in a feeling of completeness; which seldom abides
with fulness of possession, and never stops with
self, but always inspires to some great work of

love and sacrifice — as in such a case there can
be no religious life, he fully realizes the poet's
description of the splendor and the wretchedness
of him who

> " * * built his soul a costly pleasure-house,
>   Wherein at ease for aye to dwell ;"

and who said

> " * * O soul, make merry and carouse,
>   Dear soul, for all is well.
>   *   *   *   *   *
> " Singing and murmuring in her feastful mirth,
>   Joying to feel herself alive,
>   Lord over nature, lord of the visible earth,
>   Lord of the senses five ;
>
> " Communing with herself: ' All these are mine,
>   And let the world have peace or wars,
>   'Tis one to me,' * * * * *
>
> " * * * * * So three years
>   She throve, but on the fourth she fell,
>   Like Herod, when the shout was in his ears,
>   Struck through with pangs of hell."

The truth is, there is no one place, however

we may envy it, which would be indisputably good for us to occupy; much less for us to remain in. The zest of life, like the pleasure which we receive from a work of art, or from nature, comes from undulations — from inequalities; not from any monotony, even though it be the monotony of seeming perfection. The beauty of the landscape depends upon contrasts, and would be lost in one common surface of splendor. The grandeur of the waves is in the deep hollows, as well as the culminating crests; and the bars of the sunset glow on the back-ground of the twilight. The very condition of a great thing is that it must be comparatively a rare thing. We speak of summer glories, and yet who would wish it to be always summer? — who does not see how admirably the varied seasons are fitted to our appetite for change? It may seem as if it would be pleasant to have it always sunshine; and yet when fruit and plant are dying from lack of moisture, and the earth sleeps exhausted in the torrid air, who ever saw a summer morning more beautiful than that when the clouds muster their legions to the sound of the thunder, and pour upon us the blessing of the rain? We repine at toil, and yet how gladly do we turn in from the lapse of recreation to the harness of effort! We sigh for the freedom and glory of the country; but, in due time, just as fresh and beautiful seem to us the brick walls and the busy streets where our lot is cast, and our interests run. There is no condition in life of which we can say exclusively "It is good for us to be here." Our course is appointed through vicissitude, — our discipline is in alternations; and we can build no abiding tabernacles along the way.

But, I observe, in the second place, that there are those who may discard the notion of retaining any particular condition of life, and yet they would preserve unbroken some of its *relations*. They may not keep the freshness of youth, or prevent the intrusion of trouble, or shut out the

claims of responsibility, or the demands for effort;
— they may not achieve anything of this kind;
and they do not wish to achieve it; but they
would build a tabernacle to LOVE, and keep the
objects of dear affection safe within its enclosure.
"Joy, sorrow, poverty, riches, youth, decay, —
let these come as they must," say they, "in the
flow of Providence; but let the heart's sanctuaries
remain unbroken, and let us in all this change
find the presence and the ministration of those
we love." And, common as the sight is, we
must always contemplate with a fresh sadness
this sundering of family bonds; this cancelling
of the dear realities of home; this stealing in
of the inevitable gloom; this vacating of the
chair, the table, and the bed; this vanishing of
the familiar face into darkness; this passage from
communion to memory; this diminishing of love's
orb into narrower phases, — into a crescent, —
into a shadow. Surely, however broad the view
we take of the universe, a real woe, a veritable

experience of suffering amidst this boundless be-
nificence, reaching as deep as the heart's core, —
is this old and common sorrow; — the sorrow of
woman for her babes, and of man for his help-
mate, and of age for its prop, and of the son for
the mother that bore him, and of the heart for
the hearts that once beat in sympathy, and of
the eyes that hide vacancies with tears. When
these old stakes are wrenched from their sockets,
and these intimate cords are snapped, one begins
to feel his own tent shake and flap in the wind
that comes from eternity, and to realize that
there is no abiding tabernacle here.

But ought we really to wish that these relations might remain unbroken, and to murmur
because it is not so? We shall be able to answer
this question in the negative, I think, — however
hard it may be to do so, — when we consider, in
the first place, that this breaking up and separation are inevitable. For we may be assured that
whatever in the system of things *is* inevitable is

beneficent. The dissolution of these bonds comes by the same law as that which ordains them; and we may be sure that the one — though it plays out of sight, and is swallowed up in mystery — is as wise and tender in its purpose as the other. It is very consoling to recognize the Hand that gave in the Hand that takes a friend, and to know that he is borne away in the bosom of Infinite Gentleness, as he was brought here. It is the privilege of angels, and of a faith that brings us near the angels, to *always* behold the face of our Father in Heaven; and so we shall not desire the abrogation of this law of dissolution and separation. We shall strengthen ourselves to contemplate the fact that the countenances we love must change, and the ties that are closest to our hearts will break; and we shall feel that it *ought* to be, because it *must* be, — because it is an inevitability in that grand and bounteous scheme in which stars rise and set, and life and death play into each other.

But, even within the circle of our own knowledge, there is that which may reconcile us to
these separations, and prevent the vain wish of
building perpetual tabernacles for our human love.
For who is prepared, at any time, to say that it
was not better for the dear friend, and better for
ourselves, that he should go, rather than stay; —
better for the infant to die with flowers upon its
breast, than to live and have thorns in its heart;
— better to kiss the innocent lips that are still
and cold, than to see the living lips that are
scorched with guilty passion; — better to take
our last look of a face while it is pleasant to
remember — serene with thought, and faith, and
many charities — than to see it toss in prolonged
agony, and grow hideous with the wreck of intellect?   And, as spiritual beings, — placed here not
to be gratified, but to be trained, — surely we
know that often it is the drawing up of these
earthly ties that draws up our souls; that a great
bereavement breaks the crust of our mere animal

consciousness, and inaugurates a spiritual faith; and we are baptized into eternal life through the cloud and the shadow of death.

But, once more, I remark, that there are those who may say, "We do not ask for any permanence in the conditions of life; we do not ask that even its dearest relationships should be retained; but give, O! give us ever those highest, brightest moods of *faith* and of *truth*, which constitute the glory of religion, and lift us above the conflict and the sin of the world!" No truly religious mind can fail to perceive the gravitation of its thoughts and desires, and the contrast between its usual level and its best moments of contemplation and prayer. And it may indeed seem well to desire the prolongation of these experiences; to desire to live ever in that un-worldly radiance, close to the canopy of God, — in company with the great and the holy, — in company with the apostles and with Jesus, — on some Mount of Transfiguration, in garments whiter than snow, and with faces bright as the sun; and the hard, bad, trying world far distant and far below. Does not the man of spiritual sensitiveness envy those sainted ones who have grown apart, in pure clusters, away above the sinful world, blossoming and breathing fragrance on the very slopes of heaven?

. And yet, is *this* the complete ideal of life? and is this the way in which we are to accom - plish its true end? I think we may safely say that even the brightest realizations of religion should be comparatively rare, otherwise we. forget the work and lose the discipline of our mortal lot. The great saints — the men whose names stand highest in the calendar of the church universal — are not the ascetics, not the contemplators, not the men who walked apart in cloisters; but those who came down from the Mount of Communion and Glory, to take a part in the world; who have carried its burdens in their souls, and its scars upon their breasts; who have wrought for its deepest interests, and died for its highest good; whose garments have swept its common ways, and whose voices have thrilled in its low places of suffering and of need; — men who have leaned lovingly against the world, until the motion of their great hearts jars in its pulses forever; men who have gone up from dust, and blood, and crackling fire; men with faces of serene endurance and lofty denial, yet of broad, genial, human sympathies; — these are the men who wear starry crowns, and walk in white robes, yonder.

We need our visions for inspiration, but we must work in comparative shadow; otherwise, the very highest revelations would become monotonous, and we should long for still higher. And yet, are there not some whose desire is for constant revelation? Who would see supernatural sights, and hear supernatural sounds, and know all the realities towards which they are drifting, as well as those in which they must work? They would make this world a mount of *perpetual* vision; overlooking the fact that it has its own purposes, to be wrought out by its own light, and within its own limits. For my part, I must confess that I do not share in this desire to know all about the next world, and to see beforehand everything that is going to be. I have no *solicitude* about the mere scenery and modes of the future state. But this desire to be in the midst of perpetual revelations argues that there is not enough to fill our minds and excite our wonder here; when all things around us are pregnant with suggestion, and invite us, and offer unfathomed depths for our curious seeking. There is so much here, too, for our love and our discipline; so much for us to *do*, that we hardly need more revelations just now; — they might overwhelm and disturb us in the pursuit of these appointed ends. Moreover, the gratification of this desire would foreclose that glorious anticipation, that trembling expectancy, which is so fraught with inspiration and delight, — the joy of the unknown,

— the bliss of the thought that there is a great deal yet to be revealed.

We do need some revelation; just such as has been given; — a glimpse of the immortal splendors; an articulate Voice from heaven — a view of the glorified Jesus; a revelation in a point of *time*, just as that on the mount was in point of *space*. We need some; but not too much, — not *all* revelation; not revelation as a *customary fact.* If so, I repeat, we should neglect this ordained field of thought and action. We should live in a sphere of supernaturalism, — in an atmosphere of wonder, — amid a planetary roll of miracles; still unsatisfied; still needing the suggestion of higher points to break the stupendous monotony.

And I insist that *work*, not *vision*, is to be the ordinary method of our being here, against the position of those who shut themselves in to a contemplative and extatic piety. They would escape from the age, and its anxieties; they would recall past conditions; they would get into the shadow of cloisters, and build cathedrals for an exclusive sanctity. And, indeed, we would do well to consider those tendencies of our time which lead us away from the inner life of faith and prayer. But this we should cherish, not by withdrawing all sanctity from life, but by pouring sanctity into life. We should not quit the world, to build tabernacles in the Mount of Transfiguration, but come from out the celestial brightness, to shed light into the world, — to make the whole earth a cathedral; to overarch it with Christian ideals, to transfigure its gross and guilty features, and fill it with redeeming truth and love.

Surely, the lesson of the incident connected with the text is clear, so far as the apostles were concerned, who beheld that dazzling brightness, and that heavenly companionship, apart on the mount. *They* were not permitted to remain apart; but were dismissed to their appointed work. Peter went to denial and repentance, — to toil and martyrdom; James to utter his practical truth; John to send the fervor of his spirit among the splendors of the Apocalypse, and, in its calmer flow through his Gospel, to give us the clearest mirror of the Saviour's face.

Nay, even for the Redeemer that was not to be an abiding vision; and he illustrates the purport of life as he descends from his transfiguration to toil, and goes forward to exchange that robe of heavenly brightness for the crown of thorns.

What if Jesus had *remained* there, upon that Mount of Vision, and himself stood before us as only a transfigured form of glory? Where then would be the peculiarity of his work, and its effect upon the world?

On the wall of the Vatican, untarnished by the passage of three hundred years, hangs the master-piece of Raphael, — his picture of the Transfiguration. In the centre, with the glistening raiment and the altered countenance, stands

3

the Redeemer. On the right hand and on the left are his glorified visitants; while, underneath the bright cloud, lie the forms of Peter, and James, and John, gazing at the transfigured Jesus, shading their faces as they look. Something of the rapture and the awe that attracted the apostles to that shining spot seems to have seized the soul of the great artist, and filled him with his greatest inspiration. But he saw what the apostles, at that moment, did not see, and, in another portion of his picture, has represented the scene at the foot of the hill, — the group that awaited the descent of Jesus. The poor possessed boy, writhing, and foaming, and gnashing his teeth, — his eyes, as some say, in their wild, rolling agony, already catching a glimpse of the glorified Christ above; the baffled disciples, the cavilling scribes, the impotent physicians, the grief-worn father, seeking in vain for help. Suppose Jesus had *stayed* upon the mount, what would have become of that group of want, and helplessness, and agony? Suppose Christ had remained in the brightness of that vision forever, — himself only a vision of glory, and not an example of toil, and sorrow, and suffering, and death, — alas! for the great world at large, waiting at the foot of the hill; — the groups of humanity in all ages; — the sin-possessed sufferers; the cavilling sceptics; the philosophers, with their books and instruments; the bereaved and frantic mourners in their need!

So, my hearers, wrapped in the higher moods of the soul, and wishing to abide among upper glories, *we* may not see the work that waits for us along our daily path; without doing which all our visions are vain. We *must* have the visions. We need them in our estimate of the world around us, — of the aspects and destinies of humanity. There are times when justice is balked, and truth covered up, and freedom trampled down; — when we may well be tempted to ask, " What is the use of trying to work?" — when we may well inquire whether what we are doing *is* work at all. And in such a case, or in any other, one is lifted up, and inspired, and enabled to do and to endure all things, when in steady vision he beholds the ever-living God, — when all around the injustice, and conflict, and suffering of the world, he detects the Divine Presence, like a bright cloud overshadowing. O! then doubt melts away, and wrong dwindles, and the jubilee of victorious falsehood is but a peal of drunken laughter, and the spittings of guilt and contempt no more than flakes of foam flung against a hero's breast-plate. Then one sees, as it were, with the vision of God, who looked down upon the old cycles, when a sweltering waste covered the face of the globe, and huge, reptile natures held it in dominion; — who beholds the pulpy worm, down in the sea, building the pillars of continents; — so one sees the principalities of evil sliding from their thrones, and the deposits of humble faithfulness rising from the deep of ages. Our sympathy, our benevolent effort in the work of God and humanity, how much do they need not only the vision of intellectual foresight, but of the faith which, on bended knees, sees further than the telescope!

And alas! for him who, in his *personal* need and effort, has no margin of holier inspiration — no rim of divine splendor — around his daily life! Without the vision of life's great realities we cannot see what our work is, or know how to do it.

But such visions must be necessarily rare and transient, or we shall miss their genuine efficacy. We must work in comparative shadow, without the immediate sight of these realities; and only in the place of our rest, — rest for higher efforts and a new career, — only *there* may we have their constant companionship, and build their perpetual tabernacles.

The Shadow of Disappointment.

The Shadow of Disappointment.

But we trusted that it had been he which should have redeemed Israel. LUKE xxiv. 21.

IN the accounts of the disciples, contained in the New Testament, there is no attempt to glorify them, or to conceal any weakness. From the first to the last, they think and act precisely as men would think and act in their circumstances; — they are affected just as others of like culture would be affected by such events as those set forth in the record. And the genuineness of their conduct argues the genuineness of the incidents which excited it. The divine, wonder-working, risen Jesus, is the necessary counterpart of the amazed, believing, erring hoping, despond-

ing, rejoicing fishermen and publicans.   This
stamp of reality is very evident in the instance
before us.   The conduct and the feelings of the
disciples are those of men who have been involved
in a succession of strange experiences.   For a
little while they have been in communion with
One who has spoken as never man spoke, and
who has touched the deepest springs of their
being.   He has lifted them out of the narrow
limits of their previous lives.   From the Receipt
of Customs, and the Galilean lake, he has summoned them to the interests and awards, the
thought and the work, of a spiritual and divine
kingdom.   At first following him, perhaps they
hardly knew why, conscious only that he had
the Words of Eternal Life, the terms of this dis-
cipleship have grown into bonds of the dearest
intimacy.   Their Master has become their Companion and their Friend, and their faith has
deepened into tender and confiding love.   But
still, theirs has been the belief of the trusting

soul, rather than the enlightened intellect. From
the fitness of the teaching, and the wonder of
the miracle, they have felt that he was the very
Christ; and yet, from this conviction of the heart
they have not been able to separate their Jewish
conceits. Sometimes, it may be, the language of
the Saviour has carried them up into a broader
and more spiritual region; but then, they have
subsided into their symbols and shadows; — only,
notwithstanding the errors that have hindered,
and the hints that have awed them, they have
steadily felt the inspiration of a great hope, —
the expectation of something glorious to be revealed in the speedy coming of the Messiah's
kingdom. And now, does not the account immediately connected with the text picture for us
exactly the state of men whose conceptions have
been broken up by a great shock, and yet in
whose hearts the central hope still remains and
vibrates with mysterious tenacity? — men who
have had the *form* of their expectation utterly

refuted and scattered into darkness, but who still
cherish its *spirit?* Christ the crowned King, —
Christ the armed Deliverer, — Christ the Avenger,
sweeping away his foes with one burst of miracle,
— is, to them, no more. They saw the multitude
seize him, and no legions came to rescue ; — they
saw him led unresistingly away ; — they saw him
condemned, abused, crucified, buried; and so, in
no sense of which they could conceive, was this
he who should have redeemed Israel. And yet
the suggestion of something still to come, — something connected with *three days,* — lingered in
their minds. And, in the midst of their despon-
dency, striking upon this very chord, the startling
rumor reached them that Christ had risen from
the dead. It was in this mood that Jesus found
the two disciples whose words I have selected for
my text; — faith and doubt, disappointment and
hope, alternating in their minds; their Jewish conceit laid prostrate in the dust, and yet the expectation of something, they knew not what, now

strangely confirmed. See how these feelings min-
gle in the passage before us. "What manner of
communications," said the undiscerned Saviour,
"are these that ye have one to another, as ye
walk, and are sad?" — "Art thou only a stranger
in Jerusalem," says one of them, "and hast not
known the things which are come to pass there in
these days?" What things? "Concerning Jesus of Nazareth," replied they, "which was a
prophet mighty in deed and word before God and
all the people: and how the chief priests and our
rulers delivered him to be condemned to death,
and have crucified him. But we trusted that it
had been he which should have redeemed Israel:
and beside all this, to-day is the third day since
these things were done. Yea, and certain women
also of our company made us astonished, which
were early at the sepulchre; and when they found
not his body, they came, saying, that they had
also seen a vision of angels, which said that he was
alive. And certain of them which were with us

went to the sepulchre, and found it even so as the women had said: but him they saw not."

My hearers, I think we see, in this instance, the minds of these disciples working as the minds of men might be expected to work under like conditions. And to me this casts a complexion of genuineness upon the transactions which, as stated in the record, *account* for these mental alternations. The entire passage is alive with reality. The genuine emotions of humanity play and thrill together there, in the shadow of the cross and the glory of the resurrection.

But, if these feelings are thus natural, the *experience* itself indicated in that portion of this verse which constitutes the text is not entirely removed from our ordinary life. The incident which occasioned these sad words was an extraordinary one; but its *moral significance*, as it now comes before us, illustrates many a passage in man's daily course. The language, as we read it, appears to be the language of disappointment;

— it was under the shadow of diappointment, though alternating with hope, that these disciples spoke; and it is to the lessons afforded by *disappointment* in the course of life that I now especially invite your attention.

And the precise point in the text, bearing upon this subject, is the fact, that while the disciples seemed to feel as though all redemption for Israel . was now hopeless, that process of redemption for Israel, and for the world, was going on through the agency of those very events which had filled them with dismay.   Even as they were speaking, in tones of sadness, about the crucified Christ, the living Christ, made perfect for his work by that crucifixion, was walking by their side.   Looking far this side of that shadow of disappointment which then brooded over them, we see all this, that *then* they did not see; but how is it with ourselves, under the frequent shadows cast by more ordinary events?   This suggestion may afford us some profitable thoughts.

I need hardly say, in the first place, that man is continually inspired by *expectation*. Every effort he makes is made in the conviction of possibility and the light of hope. This is the heart of ambition and the spring of toil. It is the balm which he applies to the wounds of misfortune. It is the key with which he tries the wards of nature. And from the morning of life to its last twilight he is always looking forward. The saddest spectacle of all — sadder even than pain, and bereavement, and death — is a man void of hope. The most abject people is a hopeless people, in whose hearts the memories of the past, and the pulses of endeavor, and the courage of faith are dead, and who crouch by their own thresholds and the crumbling tomb-stones of their fathers, and take the tyrant's will, without an incentive, and without even a dream. The most intense form in which misery can express itself is in the phrase, "I have nothing to live for." And he who can actually say, and who really feels this, *is* dead, and covered with the very pall and darkness of calamity.   But few, indeed, are they who can, with truth, say this.

But if hope or expectation is such a vital element of human experience, so does *disappointment* have its part in the mechanism of things, and, as we shall presently see, its wise and beneficial part.   For, after all, how few things correspond with the forecast of expectation!   To be sure, some results transcend our hope; but how many fall below it, — balk it, — turn out exactly opposite to it!   Among those who meet with disappointments in life, there are those who are expecting impossibilities, — whose expectations are inordinate, — are more than the nature of things will admit; or who are looking for a harvest where they have planted no seed.   They carry the dreams of youth in among the realities of the world, and its vanishing visions leave them naked and discouraged.   The light of romance, that glorified all things in the future, recedes as they ad-

vance, and they come upon rugged paths of fact,
— upon plain toil and daily care, — upon the
market and the field, and upon men as they are
in their weakness, and their selfishness, and their
mutual distrust.   Or they belong, it may be, to
that class who are too highly charged with hope;
whose sanguine notions never go by induction, but
by leaps; who never calculate the difficulties, but
only see the thing complete and rounded in imagination; — men with plenty of poetry, and no
arithmetic; whose *theories* work miracles, but
whose attempts are failures.   It is pleasant, sometimes, to meet with people like these, who, clothed
in the scantiest garments, and with only a crust
upon their tables, at the least touch of suggestion,
mount into a region of splendor.   Their poverty
all fades away; — the bare walls, the tokens of
stern want, the dusty world, are all transfigured
with infinite possibilities.   Achievement is only a
word, and fortune comes in at a stride.   The pal-
ace of beauty rises, fruits bloom in waste places,

gold drops from the rocks, and the entire movement of life becomes a march of jubilee. And
they are so *certain* this time, — the plan they now
have is so *sure* to succeed! I repeat, it is pleasant, sometimes, to have intercourse with such
men, who throw bloom and marvelousness upon
the actualities of the world, from the reservoirs of
their sanguine invention. At least, it is pleasant
to think how this faculty of unfailing enthusiasm
enables *them* to bear defeat, and to look away
from the cold face of necessity; — to think that,
while so many are trudging after the sounding
wheels and the monotonous jar of life, and lying
down by the way to die, these men are marching
buoyantly to a tune inside. And yet this is pleasant only from a hasty point of view. These people meet with disappointment, of course; and it is
sad to think how many lives have come to absolutely nothing, and are all strewn over, from boy-
hood to the grave, with the fragments of splendid
schemes. It is sad to think how all their vision-

ary Balbecs and Palmyras have been reared in a *real* desert, — the desert of an existence producing no substantial thing. And among these vanishing dreams, and on that melancholy waste, they learn, at last, the meaning of their disappointment. And, from their experience, we too may learn, that we are placed here to be not merely ideal artists, but actual toilers; not cadets of hope, but soldiers of endeavor.

But there are disappointments in life that succeed *reasonable* expectation; and these are the hardest of all to bear. I say the expectation is reasonable; and yet, very possibly, the bitterness of the disappointment comes from neglecting to consider the infirmity of all earthly things. It is hard when, not dreaming, but trying our best, we fail. It is hard to bear the burden and heat of the day, through all life's prime, and yet, with all our toil, to earn no repose for its evening hours. It is hard to accumulate a little gain, baptizing every dollar with our honest sweat, and then have it stricken from our grasp by the hand of calamity or of fraud. It is hard, when we have placed our confidence in man's honor, or his friendship, to find that we are fools, and that we have been led in among rocks and serpents. And hard indeed is it to see those who were worthy our love and our faith drop by our side, and leave us alone. This dear child, the blossom of so many hopes, — hard is it to see him die; — to fold all our expectation in his little shroud, and lay it away forever. We thought it had been he who should have comforted and blessed us, — in whose life we could have retraced the cycle of our own happiest experience, — whose unfolding faculties would have been a renewal of our knowledge, and his manhood not merely the prop but the refreshing of our age. This companion of our lot, — this wedded wife of our heart, — why taken away now? She has shared our early struggles, and tempered our anxiety with cheerful assurance. She has tasted the bitterness; we thought she would have been a partner of the joy. She has borne our fretfulness, and helped our perplexity, and shed a serene light into our gloom; we thought she would have been with us when we could pay the debt of faithfulness; when the cares of business did not press and disturb us so. We thought it was she whose voice, sweet with the music of old, deep memories, would have consoled us far along; and that, in some calm evening of life, when all the tumult of the world was still, and we were ready to go, we should go — not far apart — gently to our graves.

Such are the plans that *we* lay out, saying of this thing and of that thing, " We trusted that it would have been so." But the answer has been — disappointment. The old, ay, perhaps the most common lesson of life, is disappointment.

And now I ask, is it not an *intended* lesson? Evidently it comes in as an element in the Providential plan in which we are involved. For we see its disciplinary nature,—its wise and beneficial results in harmony with that plan. Consider whether it is not the fact, that the entire discipline of life grows out of a succession of disappointments. That youthful dream, in which life has stretched out like a sunny landscape with purple mountain-chains; — is it not well that it is broken up, and we strike upon rugged realities? Does not all the strength of manhood, and the power of achievement, and the glory of existence, depend upon these things which are not included in the young boy's vision of a happy world. Welcome, O! disappointment of our hope that life would prove a perpetual holiday. Welcome experience of the fact that blessing comes not from pleasure, but from labor! For in that experience alone was there ever anything truly great or good accomplished. We can conceive no possible way by which one can be made personally strong without his own effort; — no possible way by which the mind can be enriched and strengthened where it is *lifted* up, instead of climbing for itself; — no way, therefore, in which life could be at all a worthy achievement, if it were merely a plain of ease, instead of holding every ward of knowledge and of power under the guard of difficulty and the requisition of endeavor.

And it is equally true that the greatest successes grow out of great failures. In numerous instances the result is better that comes after a series of abortive experiences than it would have been if it had come at once. For all these successive failures induce a skill, which is so much additional power working into the final achievement. Nobody passes at once to the mastery, in any branch of science or of industry; and when he *does* become a master in his work it is evident, not only in the positive excellence of his performance, but in the sureness with which he avoids defects; and these defects he has learned by experimental failures. The hand that evokes such perfect music from the instrument has often failed in its touch, and bungled among the keys. And if a ' man derives skill from his own failures, so does he

from the failures of other men.   Every unsuccess-
ful attempt is, for him, so much work done; for
he will not go over *that* ground again, but seek
some new way.   Every disappointed effort fences
in and indicates the only possible path of success,
and makes it easier to find.   We should thank
past ages and other men, not only for what they
have left us of great things done, but for the
heritage of their failures.   Every baffled effort for
freedom contributes skill for the next attempt, and
ensures the day of victory.   Nations stripped and
bound, and waiting for liberty under the shadow
of thrones, cherish in memory not only the
achievements of their heroes, but the defeats of
their martyrs; and when the trumpet-voice shall
summon them once more, as surely it will, —
when they shall draw for the venture of freedom,
and unroll its glittering standard to the winds, —
they will avoid the stumbling-blocks which have
sacrificed the brave, and the errors which have
postponed former hopes.   In public and in private

action, it is true that disappointment is the school
of achievement, and the balked efforts are the very
agents that help us to our purpose.

And, if life itself — life as a whole — seems to
us but a series of disappointments, is not this the
very conviction we need to work out from it,
through our own experience?   Do we not need to
learn that this life itself is not sufficient, and holds
no blessing that will fill us completely, and with
which we may forever rest?   The baffled hopes of
our mortal state; — what are they but vain striv-
ings of the human soul, out of the path of its
highest good?   The wandering bird, driven against
the branches, and beaten by the storm, flutters at
last to the clear opening, by which it mounts
above the cloud, and finds its way to its home.
This life is not ordained in vain; — it is con-
stituted for a grand purpose, if through its
lessons of experience we become convinced that
this life is not all.   In the outset of our existence here, and merely from the teaching of

others, we cannot comprehend the great realities
of existence.

How the things that have grown familiar to
our eyes, and the lessons that have sounded trite
upon our ears, become fresh and wonderful, as
life turns into experience! How this very lesson
of disappointment lets us in to the deep meanings
of Scripture, for instance! The Christ of our
youth, — a personage standing mild and beautiful
upon the Gospel-page, — a being to admire and
love; how he developes to our later thought! —
how solemnly tender, how greatly real, he becomes
to us, when we cling to him in the agony of our
sorrow, and he goes down to walk with us on the
waters of the sea of death! As traditional sentiment, — as a wholesome subject for school-com-
position, — we have spoken and written of the
weariness of the world-worn heart, and the frailty
of earthly things. But, O! when our hearts have
actually become worn, and tried; when we begin
to learn that the things of this life *are* evanescent,

— are dropping away from us, and we slipping from them, — what inspiration of reality comes to us in the oft-heard invitation, " Come unto me, all ye that labor and are heavy-laden, and I will give you rest " ! What a depth of meaning, flowing from the eternal world, in the precept we have read so carelessly, — " Lay not up for yourselves treasures upon earth, where moth and rust doth corrupt, and thieves break through and steal " ! Thus the best results of life come from the defeats and the limitations that are involved with it.

And, in all this, observe how disappointment is the instrument of higher blessings. See how thus life itself suggests a higher good than life itself can yield. And so the attitude of the disciples, after the crucifixion, illustrates many experiences of our earthly lot. Those incidents which per- plexed and grieved them were securing the very results they seemed to prevent. So, in our ordi- nary life, the things that appear most adverse to us are often the most favorable.

I may say, indeed, that to any man who is rightly exercised by it, disappointment *always* brings a better result. But this statement requires that I should say, likewise, that the result of disappointment depends upon the level and quality of a man's spirit. "One thing happens alike to the wise man and the fool." But how different in texture and substance is the final result of the event! Disappointment breaks down a feeble and shallow man. There are those, again, whom it does not make better, — in fact, whom nothing, as we can see, makes better. Everything glides easily off from them. Now, it is a noble thing to see a man rise above misfortune, — a moral Prometheus, submissive to the actual will of God, but defying fate. But there are men whose very elasticity indicates the superficiality of their nature. For it is good sometimes to be sad, — good to have depth of being sufficient for misfortune to sink into, and accomplish its proper work. But the man who rightly receives the lesson of disap-

pointment, and improves by its discipline, bent as
he is on some great or good work, is impelled by
it only to a change of *method*, — never to a
change of *purpose;* and the disappointment effect-
ually serves the purpose.   But the fact before us
is most clearly seen when we contemplate the
results of disappointment upon a religious and an
un-religious spirit.   A man is not made better by
disappointment to whom this world is virtually
everything; — to whom spiritual things are not
realities.   To him life is a narrow stream between
jutting crags, and its substance flows away with
the objects before his eyes.   Nay, some men of
this sort are made worse by the failure of earthly
hopes, and their natures are compressed and ham-
mered by misfortune into a sullen and granitic
defiance.   But he who sees beyond these material
limits, looking to the great end and final relations
of our being, always extracts from mortal disappointment a better result.   In the wreck of external things he gathers that spiritual good which is

the substance of all life;—that faith, and patience, and holy love, which, when all that is mortal and incidental in our humanity passes away, constitute the residuum of personality.

Our hopes disappointed, — *our* plans thwarted and overthrown; but out of that disappointment a richer good evolving than we had conceived; something that tends more than all our effort to produce the real object of life. — My friends, what do we make out of this fact? Why, surely this, that *life is not our plan, but God's.* Consider what we, often, would have made out of life, and compare this with what Providence has made out of it. Contrast the man's achievement with the boy's scheme; the dream of care with the moral glory that has sprung from toil and trouble. Contrast the idea of the Saviour in the minds of those disciples with the actual Saviour rising victorious from the conditions of shame and death.

Life is God's plan; not ours. We may find this out only by effort; but we do find it out.

We are responsible for the use of our materials, but the materials themselves, and the great movement of things, are furnished for us. Let us fall into no ascetic view of life. Out of our joy and our acknowledged good the Supreme Disposer works his spiritual ends. But, especially, how often does he do this out of our trials, and sorrows, and so-called evils! Once more I say life is God's plan; not ours. For often on the ruins of visionary hope rises the kingdom of our substantial possession and our true peace; and under the shadow of earthly disappointment, all unconsciously to ourselves, our Divine Redeemer is walking by our side.

Life a Tale.

5

Life a Tale.

We spend our years as a tale that is told. PSALM xc. 9.

WE bring our years to an end like a thought, is the proper rendering of these words, according to an eminent translator. But as the essential idea of the Psalmist is preserved in the common version, I employ it as peculiarly illustrative and forcible. It will be my object, in the present discourse, to show the fitness of the comparison in the text; — to suggest the points of resemblance between human life and a passing narrative.

I observe, then, in the first place, that the propriety of this simile is seen in the *brevity* of life. What more rapid and momentary than a *story?*

It is heard, and passes. Though it beguiles us for the time, it dies away in sound, or melts from before the eye. And this, I say, strikingly illustrates the brevity of life. *The brevity of life!* It is a trite truth, and yet how little realized! Probably there is nothing more common, and yet there is nothing more pernicious, than the habit of virtual dependence upon length of days. Thus the best ends of our mortal being are lost sight of; the solemn circumstances, the suggestive mysteries of life, are misconstrued. The heavens, which give a myriad hints of worlds beyond the grave, are, to many, impenetrable walls, shutting them in to mere pursuits of sense, — the upholstery of a workshop or bazaar; and this earth, which is but a step, — a filmy platform of our immortal course, — is to them the solid abiding place of all interest, and of all hope.

It is well, then, to break in upon this worldly reliance, — to consider how fleeting and uncertain are the things in which we garner up so much.

Therefore, in order that we may more vividly *realize* the brevity of life, — how like it is to a passing tale, — let us consider the rapidity of its changes, even in a few short years. We are, to some degree, made aware how fast the current of time bears us on, when we pause and remark the shores; when we observe how our position to-day has shifted from what it was yesterday; how the sunny slopes of youth have been changed for the teeming uplands of maturity; yea, perhaps, how already the stream is narrowing, and rushing more swiftly as it narrows, towards those high hills that bound our present vision, upon whose summits lingers the departing light, and around whose base thickens the solemn shadow.

This rapidity of change is most strikingly illustrated when, after a few years' absence, we return to the scenes of our youth. We plunged into the current of the world, buoyant and vigorous; our thoughts have been occupied every hour, and we have not noticed the stealthy shadow of time.

But we come back to that early spot, and look around. Lo! the companions of our youth have grown into dignified men, — the active and influential citizens of the place. Care has set

"Busy wrinkles round their eyes."

They meet us with formal deportment, or with an ill-concealed restlessness, as though we hindered them in their work, — *work!* which, when we parted with them, would have been flung to the winds for any idle sport. How quickly they have changed into this gravity and anxiety! On the other hand, those who stood where they stand now, — whose names occupied the signs and the records which theirs now fill, — have passed away, or, here and there, come tottering along, bent and gray-headed men. Those, too, who were mere infants — those whom we never saw — take up our old stations, and inspire them with the gladness of childhood. And exactly thus have *we* changed to others. We are a mirror to them, and they to us.

From this familiar experience, then, let us *realize* that the stream of life does not stop, nor are we left stationary, but carried with it; though our condition may appear unchanged, until we lift up our eyes, and look for the old landmarks. The *brevity of our life!* my friends. Amid our daily business, — in the sounding tumult of the great mart, and the absorption of our thoughts, — do we think of it? Do we perceive how nearly we approach a goal which a little while ago seemed far before us? Do we observe how quickly we shoot by it? Do we mark with what increasing swiftness the line of our life seems reeling off, and how close we are coming to the end? Time never stops! Each tick of the clock echoes our advancing footsteps. The shadow of the dial falls upon a shorter and a shorter tract, which we have yet to pass over. Even if a long life lies before us, let us consider that thirty-five years is high noon with us, — the meridian of that arc which comprehends but threescore years and ten!

But we may be more vividly impressed with the fact of the brevity of life, if we adopt some criterion wider than these familiar measurements. The narrative, the story, engages our ears, in the pauses of care and labor. We listen to it in the noonday rest, and around the evening fire. It is a slight break in the monotony of our business, — an interlude in the solemn march of life. And thus, in some respects, is life itself. It is so, if we take into view a long series of existence, such as the succession of human generations, or, still more, the periods of creative development, and the computations of time as applied to the forms and changes of the material universe. In this vast train of being, our individual existence, however important to ourselves, is but an interlude — a tale. Let us, then, for a while, lay aside any *conventional* method of estimating our life, — a method in which that life fills a large space,

simply because it is brought near to the eye, —
and let us endeavor to take a view of it, as it
were, from the fixed stars, or from the elevation
of the immortal state.

Compare, then, if you will, this life of yours or
mine, not with the personal standard of threescore
years and ten, but with the whole course of *human history;* and instantly we appear but as
bubbles in the stream of ages. But, again, consider how history itself is as "a tale that is told;"
and then, indeed, what a mere incident in it all is
your life and mine! If we stand off at the distance of a few centuries, so that we have no
present interest in them, it is strange how the
proudest empires assume an empty and spectral
aspect. Their growth and decline occupied ages;
but what a brief achievement it appears now!
Why puzzle ourselves about their origin, or seek
to disengage the true from the fabulous in their
history? Why strain laboriously to settle names,
and dates, and dynasties? What a mere point

they have occupied in the processes of the great universe! Their hieroglyphic pillars, their gray old pyramids; — what are they to the age of Uranus, or the new planet? Each of these empires fulfilled its mission, and *relatively* that mission was a great one; but in the long sweep of God's providence, and among the phenomena of absolute being, what a brief link, a subordinate climax, it was! The huge ribs of the earth, and the coral islands of the sea, were longer in building; and even these are transitory manifestations of God's purposes, which stream around us through constant change and succession. And what, then, are these nations — these epochs of humanity — but waves rising and breaking on the great sea of eternity? Mysterious Egypt, haughty Assyria, glorious Greece, kingly Rome; — how spectral they have become. They stand out in no relief. As we recede from them, they sink back, flat and inanimate, on the horizon. Each is a tale that has been told. Surely, then, if such is the life of

nations, I need not labor to impress upon you a
sense of the brevity of our individual existence.

But, for a moment, turn your thoughts to estimates that far exceed the periods of history, and
confound all our ordinary measurements. What
is our mortal existence, into which we crowd so
much interest, — over the anticipated length of
which we slumber, — into whose uncertain future
we project our little plans so confidently, — compared to the age of the *heavens*, — the lifetime of
worlds? — compared to their march, from the
moment when they obeyed the creative fiat to that
when they shall complete their great cycle? It
takes three years for light to travel from the
nearest fixed star to the earth; from another it
takes twelve years; while, on its journey from a
star of the twelfth magnitude, twenty-four billions
of miles away, it consumes four thousand years.
And yet we speak of *long* life! Why, when
the light that wraps us now shall be changed for
the light that is just leaping from that distant

star, where in the gray bosom of the past shall *we*
be ?   Sunken, forgotten, crumbled to impercepti-
ble atoms; the ashes of generations — the dust of
empires — heaped over us !   And when we compare these wide estimates to that divine eternity
that evolves and limits all things, how does our
individual existence on the earth dwindle and
vanish ! — a heart-throb in the pulses of universal
life, — a quivering leaf in the forest of being, —
" a tale that is told " !

And yet, my friends, our realization of existence is so intense, — the horizon of the present
shuts us in so completely, — that it really requires
an effort for us to pause and remember that we *are*
such transitory beings.   It cannot be (we may
unconsciously reason), that we to whom this earth
is bound with ligaments so intimate and strong;
whose breathing and motion — whose contact and
action here — are such realities; whose ears hear
these varying sounds of life; whose eyes drink in
this perpetual and changing beauty; to whom

business, study, friendship, pleasure, domestic relations, are such fresh and constant facts; to whom
the dawn and the twilight, the nightly slumber
and the daily meal, are such regular experiences;
to whom our possessions, our houses, lands, goods,
money, are such substantial things; — it cannot be
that we are not fixed permanently here, — that
the years, like a swift river, sweep us nearer and
nearer to a point where we must sink and leave
it all, — that. the corridors of the earth echo our
footsteps only as the footsteps of a successive
march — myriads going before, and myriads coming after us — and soon they will catch no more
the murmurs of our individual life; for that will
be as "a tale that is told."

The whole train of thought I am now pursuing
strikes us with peculiar force, in reading the biog-
raphies of men who have lived intensely, who have
realized the fulness of life, who have mingled
intimately with its varied experiences, and occupied a large place in it. We see how to them

life was, as it is to us, an absorbing fact, — how
they have planned, and thought, and acted, as
though they were to live forever; and yet we have
noticed the premonitions of change, the dropping
away of friends, the failing of vigor, the deepening
of melancholy shadows, and the coming of the
end; the business closed, the active curiosity and
intermeddling ceased, the familiar haunts abandoned, the home made desolate, the lights put out,
the cup fallen beneath the festal board, and all
that earnest existence stopped forever.   And this,
too, so quick, — filling so small a space in absolute
time !   From their illustration let us, then, realize that *our* life, too, amid all these real conditions, is unfolding rapidly to an end, and is "as
a tale that is told."

But life is like a tale that is told, because of its
comprehensiveness.   It is a common characteristic of a narrative that it contains a great deal in
a small compass.   It includes many years, and
expresses many results.   Sometimes it sweeps over

different lands, and exhibits the peculiarities of various personages. In one word, it is character- ized by *comprehensiveness*. And this, I repeat, is also a characteristic of human life. When the consideration of the brevity of our mortal existence excites us to diligence it is well; but when we make it an argument for indolence, disgust, and despair, we should be reminded of the fact I am now endeavoring to illustrate, — the fact that even the briefest life contains a great deal, and means a great deal; and that, if we estimate things by a *spiritual* standard, a man's earthly being may contain more than all the cycles of the material world. From the best point of view, life is not merely a term of years and a span of action; it is a force, a current and depth of being. Indeed, considered in its most *literal* sense, as the vital spark of our animal organism, it is something more than a measurement of time; — it is a mysterious, informing essence. No man has yet been able to tell us what it is, where it resides, or how it acts.

We only know that when we gaze upon the features of the dead we see there the same *organs* that pertained to the living; but *something* has gone, — something of light, power, motion; and that something we call *life*.

But it is chiefly in a *moral* sense that I make the remark that life is something more than a term of years, or a span of action. In fact, life is *a sum of spiritual experiences;* and thus one act, or result, often contains more than a century of time. Who does not understand the fact to which I now refer? Who has not felt something of it? Has not each one of us, at times, realized that he lived a year in a single day, — in a moment, — in an emotion or thought? Nay, could that experience be measured by any estimate of time? And if we should compute the length of any life by such experiences, and not by a succession of years, would it not be a long life? At least, would it not be a full and immeasurable life?

But, while every man's history will furnish instances of what I mean, let us, for the sake of
clearer illustration, consider some of the experiences which are common to all. Defining life to
be depth and intensity of being, then, — a current
of spiritual power, and not a mere. succession of
incidents, — *how much* we live when we acquire
the knowledge of a single *truth!* What an inex-
haustible power! — what an immeasurable experience it is! We are made absolutely stronger by
it; we receive more life with it, — a new and im-
perishable fibre of being. Fortune cannot pluck it
from us, age cannot weaken it, death cannot set
limits to it. And now, with the fulness of this
one experience as a test, just consider our whole
mortal experience as filled up with such revelations
of truth. Suppose we improve all our opportunities; into what boundless life does education admit
us, and the discoveries of every day, and the ordinary lessons of the world! Tell me, is this
life to be called merely a brief and worthless fact,

6

when by a little *reading*, for instance, I can make the experience of other men, and lands, and ages, all mine? When, in some favored hour, I can climb the starry galaxy with Newton, and pace along the celestial coast to the great harmony of numbers, and unlock the mighty secret of the universe? When of a winter's night, I can pass through all the belts of climate, and all the grades of civilization on our globe; scan its motley races, learn its diverse customs, and hear the groaning of lonely ice-fields and the sigh of Indian palms? When, with Bacon, I can explore the laboratory of nature, or, with Locke, consult the mysteries of the soul? When Spencer can lead me into golden visions, or Shakspeare smite me with magic inspiration, or Milton bathe me in immortal song? When History opens for me all the gates of the past, — Thebes and Palmyra, Corinth and Carthage, Athens with its peerless glory, and Rome with its majestic pomp? — when kings and statesmen, authors and priests, with their public deeds and secret thoughts, are mine? When the plans of cabinets, and the debates of parliaments, and the course of revolutions, and the results of battle, are all before my eyes, and in my mind? When I can enter the inner chamber of sainted souls, and conspire with the efforts of moral heroes, and understand the sufferings of martyrs? Say, when all these deep experiences — these comprehensive truths — may be acquired through merely *one* privilege, is life but a dream, or a breath of air? Thus, too, do immeasurable experiences flow in to me from nature, — from planet, flower, and ocean. Thus, too, does more life come to me from contacts in the common round of action. And, I repeat, every truth thus gained expands a moment of time into illimitable being, — positively enlarges my existence, and endows me with a quality which time cannot weaken or destroy.

Consider, again, how much we really live *in cherishing good affections*, and in performing *noble deeds.* We have the familiar lines of the poet, to this point :

> " One self-approving hour whole years outweighs
> Of stupid starers and of loud huzzas."

It is true. There *is* more life in one "self-approving hour," — one act of benevolence, — one work of self-discipline, — than in threescore years and ten of mere sensual existence. Go out among the homes of the poor, lift up the disconsolate, administer comfort to the forlorn; in some way, as it may come across your path, or lie in the sphere of your duty, do a deed of kindness; and in that one act you shall live more than in a year of selfish indulgence and indolent ease, — yea, more than in a lifetime of such. The poet, with his burning, immortal lines, while doing his work, lives all the coming ages of his fame. From every marble feature that he chisels, the sculptor draws an intensity of being that cannot be imparted by a mere extension of years. The philanthropist, in his walks of mercy and his ministrations of love, lives more comprehensively than another may in a century. His is the fathomless bliss of benevolence, — the experience of God. The martyr, in his dying hour, with his face shining like an angel's, does not live longer, but he lives *more*, than all his persecutors.

Consider, too, the experiences of religion, of worship, of prayer. In the act of communion with God, in the realization of immortality, in the aspirations and the idea of perfection, there is a depth and scope of being from which all sensual estimates of time drop away.

Our mortal life, then, is very *comprehensive*. If we measure it, not by its length of years, but by its *spiritual results*, be they good or evil, it is a full and large life. It then appears, like the immortal state, not as a fact of succession, but of *experience*. Christ has defined eternal life as such a fact. "Eternal life," he says, "is to know thee, the only true God, and Jesus Christ whom thou hast sent." The life of the blessed in heaven is not marked by years and cycles; it is not so much protracted being, as a power of knowledge, — a depth of glad and holy consciousness, — a constant pulsation of harmony with God.

Again, every life may be compared to "a tale that is told," because it has a *plot*. In the narrative there is a combination of agencies working to a crisis. There is a *main-point* with which all the action is involved. And so every human life has its main-point. I will not now take up time to carry out this illustration minutely. The mere suggestion that each one is working out a peculiar destiny invests even the meanest life with a solemn dignity, and counteracts any disparaging argument drawn from its brevity.

But still I would urge, that the propriety of this comparison between the peculiar tendency of an individual life and the plot of a story, is seen in the fact that every man is accomplishing a certain moral result in and for himself. This is inevitable. We may be inactive, but that result is forming; the mould of habit is growing, and the inward life is unfolding itself, after its kind. We may think our career is aimless, but all things give a shape to our character. And does not this consideration make our mortal life of deep consequence to us?

All circumstances and experiences are chiefly important as affecting this result. One of the highest views we can take of the universe is that of a theatre for the soul's education. We are placed upon this earth not to be absorbed by it, but to use it for the highest spiritual occasions. We are placed among the joys and sorrows of our daily lives to be trained for immortal issues. Our business, our domestic duties, and all our various relations, constitute a school for our souls. Here our affections and our powers are acted upon for good or for evil. Grief strengthens our faith and elevates our thoughts; joy quickens our gratitude, our obedience, and our trust; temptation forms in us an exalted and spontaneous virtue, or enfeebles and enslaves us. Chiefly, then, should we be solicitous about character, the plot of our life; and in this solicitude our earthly existence rises to the highest importance.

Let us, then, feel that our mortal career is not vague and aimless. Let us realize that each life is a special history. The poorest, the most obscure, has such a history; and although it may be unnoticed by men, angels regard it with interest. The merchant, every day, in the dust, and heat, and busy maze of traffic, unfolds a history. The beggar by the way-side, it may be, outrivals kings in the grandeur and magnitude of *his* history. In sainted homes, — in narrow nooks of life, — in the secret heart of love, and prayer, and patience, — many a tale is told which God alone sees, and which he approves. The needy tell a tale, in their unrelieved wants and unpitied sufferings. The oppressed tell a tale, that goes up into the ears of the Lord of Sabaoth. The vicious tell a tale of wo, and misspent opportunity, and wasted power. Let us think of it, I beseech you! Each one of us in his sphere of action is developing a plot which surely tells in character, — which is fast running into a great fixed fact.

Once more, we may compare every life to "a tale that is told," because it has a *moral.* Any story, good or bad, — the most pernicious work of fiction, the most flimsy narrative, as the grandest history, — has its significance. ' So it is with the life of a man. As in all his conduct he is building up the intrinsic results of character for himself, — establishing in his own soul a fabric of welfare or of wo, — so is he furnishing a lesson for *others*, and accomplishing an end by which *they* are affected. The purpose for which any one has lived, the point which he has attained, the personal history which he has unfolded, constitute the moral of his life.

For instance, here is a man whose life is *frivolous*, — divided between aimless cares and super-

ficial enjoyments.   He has no resources in himself,
no fountain of inward peace and joy.   His spirit
leaps like new wine in the whirl of exciting pleasure, but in the hour of solitude and of golden
opportunity, it is "flat, stale, and unprofitable."
He marks off the year by its festivals, and distrib-
utes the day into hours of food, rest, and folly.
In short, he holds no serious conception of life, and
he is untouched by lofty sentiment.   The great
drama of existence, with its solemn shifts of scenery
and its impending grandeur, is but a pantomime to
him; and he a thoughtless epicurean, a grinning
courtier, a scented fop, a dancing puppet, on the
mighty stage.   And surely, such a life, a life of
superficiality and heartlessness, a life of silken
niceties and conventional masquerade, a life of
sparkling effervescence, has a *moral*.   It shows us
how vain is human existence when empty of
serious thought, of moral purpose, and of devout
emotion.

Another is a *skeptic*.   He has no genuine faith

in immortality, in virtue, or in God. To him, life is
a sensual opportunity closing up with annihilation,
and to be enjoyed as it may. It is a mere game,
and he who plays the most skilful hand will win.
Virtue is a smooth decency, which it is well to
assume in order to cover an artful selfishness; and
it is a noteworthy fact, too, that, in the long run,
those who have trusted to virtue have made by it.
At least, vice is inexpedient, and it will not do to
make a public profession of it. Religion, too, he
says, is well enough; it does for the weak and the
ignorant; though *shrewd* men, like our skeptic,
know that it is all a sham, and, of course, scarce
give it a serious thought. What is religion to a
keen-minded, hard-headed, sagacious man of the
world? What has it to do with business, and
politics, and such practical matters? Pack it
away for Sunday, and then put it on with clean
clothes, out of respect for the world; but if it lifts
any remonstrance in the caucus or the counting-
room, why, like a *shrewd* man, laugh it out of

countenance. What has our skeptic to do with the future world or with spiritual relations? Keep bugbears to frighten more timid and credulous persons. But only see how *he* uses the world, and plays his scheme, and foils his adversary, and twists and bends his plastic morality, all because he is not troubled with scruples, and has no faith in God or duty!

And yet, to the serious eye, that scans his spiritual mood, and looks all around his shrewd, self-confident position, there is a great *moral* in that skeptic's life. It teaches us, more than ever, the value of faith, and the glory of religion. That flat negation only makes the rejected truth more positive. That specimen of what existence is without God in the world, causes us to yearn more earnestly for the shelter of His presence, and the blessedness of His control. From the dark perspective of the skeptic's sensual view, the bleak annihilation that bounds all his hopes, we turn more gladly to the auroral promise of immortality, to the consolations and influences of a life beyond the grave. Yes, in that tale that is told, in that skeptic history, there is indeed a great moral. It shows how meaningless and how mean, how treacherous and false, is that man's life who hangs upon the balance of a cunning egotism, and moves only from the impulses of selfish desire—without religion, without virtue, repudiating the idea of morality, and practically living without God.

Or, on the other hand, suppose we call up the image of one who has well kept the trusts of family, and kindred, and friendship; — one who has made home a pleasant place; who has filled it with the sanctities of affection, and adorned it with a graceful and generous hospitality; — before whose cheerful temper the perplexities of business have been smoothed, and whose genial disposition has melted even the stern and selfish; — who, thus rendering life around her happier and better, attracting more closely the hearts of relatives, and making every acquaintance a friend, has, chief of all, beautifully discharged the sacred offices of *wife* and *mother*; encountering the day of adversity with a noble self-devotion, enriching the hour of prosperity with wise counsel and faithful love; unwearied in the time of sickness, patient and trustful beneath the dispensation of affliction; in short, by her many virtues and graces evidently the bright centre of a happy household. And now suppose that, with all these associations clinging to her, in the bloom of life, with opportunities for usefulness and enjoyment opening all around her, death interferes, and suddenly quenches that light! Is there not left a *moral* in which abides a sweet and lasting consolation? That moral is — the power of a kind heart; the worth of domestic virtues; the living freshness of a memory in which these qualities are combined.

Thus, then, in its *brevity* and its *comprehensiveness*, with its *plot* and its *moral*, we see that each human life is like "a tale that is told." To you, my friends, I leave the personal application of these truths. Surely they suggest to each of us the most vital and solemn considerations. Surely they call us to diligence and repentance, — to introspection and prayer. What we are in *ourselves*, — what use we shall make of life; — is not this an all important subject? What lesson we shall furnish for *others*, — what influence for good or evil; — can we be indifferent to that? God give us grace and strength to ponder and to act upon these suggestions!

Finally, remember under whose dominion all the sorrows and changes of earth take place. Let your faith in Him be firm and clear. To Him address your grief; — to Him lift up your prayer. Of Him seek strength and consolation; — of Him ask that a holy influence may attend every experience. And while all the trials of life should quicken us to a loftier diligence, and inspire us with a keener sense of personal responsibility, surely when our hearts are sore and bleeding, — when our hopes lie prostrate, and we are faint and troubled, it is good to rise to the contemplation of the Infinite Controller, — to lean back upon the Almighty Goodness that upholds the universe; to realize that He does verily watch over us, and care for us; to feel that around and above all things else He moves the vast circle of his purpose, and carries within it all our joys and sorrows; and that this mysterious tale of human life — this tangled plot of our earthly being — is unfolded beneath His all-beholding eye, and by His omnipotent and paternal hand.

The Christian View of Sorrow.

7

The Christian View of Sorrow.

A man of sorrows, and acquainted with grief. Is. liii. 3.

THERE is one great distinction between the productions of Heathen and of Christian art. While the first exhibits the perfection of physical form and of intellectual beauty, the latter expresses, also, the majesty of sorrow, the grandeur of endurance, the idea of triumph refined from agony. In all those shapes of old there is nothing like the glory of the martyr; the sublimity of patience and resignation; the dignity of the thorn-crowned Jesus.

It is easy to account for this. In that heathen age the soul had received no higher inspiration. It was only after the advent of Christ that men realized the greatness of sorrow and endurance. It was not until the history of the Garden, the Judgment-Hall, and the Cross had been developed, that genius caught nobler conceptions of the beautiful. This fact is, therefore, a powerful witness to the prophecy in the text, and to the truth of Christianity. Christ's personality, as delineated in the Gospels, is not only demonstrated by a change of dynasties, — an entire new movement in the world, — a breaking up of its ancient order; but the moral ideal which now leads human action, — which has wrought this enthusiasm, and propelled man thus strangely forward, — has entered the subjective realities of the soul, — breathed a new inspiration upon it, — opened up to it a new conception; and, lo! the statue dilates with a diviner expression; — lo! the picture wears a more lustrous and spiritual beauty.

The Christ of the text, then, — "A man of sorrows, and acquainted with grief," — has verily lived; for his image has been reflected in the minds of men, and has fastened itself there among their most intimate and vivid conceptions. Sorrow, as illustrated in Christ's life, and as interpreted in his scheme of religion, has assumed a new aspect, and yields a new meaning. Its garments of heaviness have become transfigured to robes of light, its crown of thorns to a diadem of glory; and often, for some one whom the rich and joyful of this world pity, — some suffering, struggling, over-shadowed soul, — comes there a voice from heaven, "This is my beloved son, in whom I am well pleased."

I remark, however, that Christianity does not accomplish this result by *denying the character* of sorrow. It does not refuse to render homage to grief. The stoic is as far from its ideal of virtue as the epicurean. The heart of the true saint quivers at pain, and his eyes are filled with tears. Whatever mortifications he may deem necessary as to the passions of this poor flesh, if he imitates the example of Christ he cannot deny those better affections which link us even to God; he cannot harden those sensitive fibres which are the springs of our best action, — which if callus we become inhuman. He realizes pain; he recognises sorrow as sorrow. Its cup is bitter, and to be resisted with prayer.

There is nothing more wonderful in the history of Jesus than his keen sense of sorrow, and the scope which he allows it. In the tenderness of his compassion he soothed the overflowing spirit, but he never rebuked its tears. On the contrary, in a most memorable instance, he recognized its right to grieve. It was on the way to his own crucifixion, when crowned with insult, and lacerated with his own sorrows. "Daughters of Jerusalem," said he, to the sympathizing women, "weep not for me, but weep for yourselves and for your children." As though he had said, "You have a right to weep; weep, then, in that great catastrophe which is coming, when barbed affliction shall pierce your hearts, and the dearest ties shall be cut in sunder. Those ties are tender; those hearts are sacred. Therefore, weep!"

But Christ did more than sanction tears in others. He wept himself. Closest in our consciousness, because they will be most vivid to us in our darkest and our last hours, are those incidents by the grave of Lazarus, and over against Jerusalem; the sadness of Gethsemane, and the divine pathos of the last supper. Never can we fully realize what a tribute to sorrow is rendered by the tears of Jesus, and the dignity which has descended upon those who mourn, because he had not where to lay his head, was despised and rejected of men, and cried out in bitter agony from the cross. He could not have been our exemplar by despising sorrow. — by treating it with contempt; but only by shrinking from its pain, and becoming intimate with its anguish, — only as " a man of sorrows, and acquainted with grief."

But, on the other hand, Christianity does not

over-estimate sorrow.   While it pronounces a benediction upon the mourner, it does not declare it best that man should always mourn.   It would not have us deny the good that is in the universe. Nay, I apprehend that sorrow itself is a testimony to that good, — is the anguish and shrinking of the severed ties that have bound us to it; that it clings closest in hearts of the widest and most various sympathies; that only souls which have loved much and enjoyed much can feel its intensity, or know its discipline.   In the language of another, " Sorrow is not an independent state of mind, standing unconnected with all others. . . . . . It is the effect, and, under the present conditions of our being, the inevitable effect, of strong affections. Nay, it is not so much their result, as a certain attitude of those affections themselves.   It not simply *flows from* the love of excellence, of wisdom, of sympathy, but it *is* that very love, when conscious that excellence, that wisdom, that sympathy, have departed."   They, then, who deem it necessary for man's spiritual welfare that he should constantly feel the pressure of chastisement, and be engirt with the mist of tears, do not reason well. Jeremy Taylor reasons thus, when he says, in allusion to certain lamps which burned for many ages in a tomb, but which expired when brought into open day : — "So long as we are in the retirements of sorrow, of want, of fear, of sickness, we are burning and shining lamps; but when God lifts us up from the gates of death, and carries us abroad into the open air, to converse with prosperity and temptations, we go out in darkness; and we cannot be preserved in light and heat but by still dwelling in the regions of sorrow." "There is beauty, and, to a certain extent, truth, in this figure," says a writer, in reply; "but it by no means follows that continuous suffering would be good for man; on the contrary, it would be as remote from producing the perfection of our moral nature as unmitigated prosperity. It would be apt to produce a morbid and ghastly piety; the 'bright lamps' of which Taylor speaks, would still be irradiating only a tomb."*   We may doubt whether there is more essential religiousness in this seeking of sorrow as a mortification, — in this monastic self-laceration and exclusion, — than in the morbid misery of the hypochondriac.   Neither comprehends the whole of life, nor is adapted to its realities. ` Christ was "a man of sorrows and acquainted with grief;" but he was also full of sympathy with all good, and enjoyed the charm of friendship, and the light of existence.   Around that great Life gather many amenities.   Below that face of agony beats a heart familiar with the best affections of human nature; otherwise, we may believe, that agony would not appear.   The sadness of that last supper indicates the breaking up of many joyful communions; and that history which closes in the shadow of the cross mingles with the festival of Cana, and lingers around the home at Bethany.

* *Edinburgh Review*, No. 141.   The article on Pascal.

But I remark, once more, that while Christianity neither despises nor affects to desire sorrow, it clearly recognizes its great and beneficial mission.   In one word, it shows its *disciplinary* character, and thus practically interprets the mystery of evil.   It regards man as a spiritual being, thrown upon the theatre of this mortal life not merely for enjoyment, but for *training*, — for the development of spiritual affinities, and the attainment of spiritual ends.   It thus reveals a weaning, subduing, elevating power, in sorrow.

The *origin* of evil may puzzle us; — its *use* no Christian can deny.   A sensual philosophy may shrink from it, in all its aspects, and retreat into a morbid scepticism or a timid submission.   If we predicate mere happiness as "our being's end and aim," there is no explanation of evil.   From this point of view, there is an ambiguity in nature, — a duality in every object, which we cannot solve.   The throne of infinite light and love casts over the face of creation an inexplicable shadow.   If we were made merely to be happy, why this hostility all around us? Why these sharp oppositions of pain and difficulty? Why these writhing nerves, these aching hearts, and over-laden eyes? . Why the chill of disappointment, the shudder of remorse, the crush and blight of hope? Why athwart the horizon flicker so many shapes of misery and sin? Why appear these sad spectacles of painful dying chambers, and weary sick-beds? — these countless tomb-stones, too — ghastly witnesses to death and tears? Explain for me these abrupt inequalities, — the long train of necessities, poverty and its kindred woes, those fearful realities that lie in the abysses of every city, — that hideous, compressed mass which welters in the awful baptism of sensuality and ignorance, — the groans of inarticulate woe, the spectacle of oppression, the shameless cruelty of war, the pestilence that shakes its comet-sword over nations, and famine that peers with skeleton face through the corn-sheaves of plenty. Upon this· theory of *mere* happiness no metaphysical subtlety can solve the fact of evil; — the coiled enigma constantly returns upon itself, inexplicable as ever.

But when we take the Christian view of life, we discover that not happiness merely, but *virtue, holiness*, is the great end of man; though happiness comes in as an inevitable consequence and accompaniment of this result. And in the light reflected from this view, evil assumes a powerful, and, I may say, a most beautiful office. It is just as necessary for the attainment of virtue as prosperity, or any blessing. Nay, in this aspect, it is itself a great blessing, and

> "Every cloud that spreads above
> And veileth love, itself is love."

It is evident that, without the contact of sin and the pressure of temptation, there might be innocence, but not virtue. Equally evident does it seem that, without an acquaintance with grief, there would be but little of that uplifting ten-

dency — that softening of the heart, and sanctifying of the affections — which fit us for the dissolution of our earthly ties, and for the communions
of the spiritual world. Beautiful is this weaning
efficacy of sorrow. By the ordinance of God,
youth is made to be content with this outward and
palpable life. The sunshine and the air — the
flow of animal pleasures, encircled mysteriously
with the guardianship of parents, and the love of
friends — are sufficient for the child. But as we
grow in years, there springs up a dissatisfaction,
a restlessness, of which we may be only half conscious, and still less know how to cure. With
some, this may subside into merely a fearful and
worldly discontent; others may heed the prophecy,
and lay hold on a celestial hope, an immortal possession, as the only remedy. In this secret sense
of want, which neither nature nor man can fill,
• they will hear already that low, divine voice, —
"Come unto me, all ye that labor and are heavy
laden, and I will give you rest." But generally

another and more emphatic missionary is necessary. It is the veiled angel of sorrow, who plucks
away one thing and another that bound us here in
ease and security, and in the vanishing of these
dear objects indicates the true home of our affections and our peace. Thus, by rupture and loss
we become weaned from earth, and the dissatisfaction and discontent which sorrow thus induces
are as kind and providential as the carelessness of
youth.

Who does not see that it is so, — that as we
journey on in life there are made in our behalf
preparations for another state of being, — unmis-
takable premonitions of that fact which the author
of the Epistle to the Hebrews so eloquently states,
that "here have we no continuing city"? The
gloss of objects in which we delighted is worn off
by attrition, — is sicklied o'er by care; the vanity
of earthly things startles us suddenly, like a new
truth; the friends we love drop away from our side
into silence; desire fails; the grasshopper becomes

a burden; until, at length, we feel that our only
love is not here below, — until these tendrils of
earth aspire to a better climate, and the weight
that has been laid upon us makes us stoop wearily
to the grave as a rest and a deliverance.   We
have, even through our tears, admired that discipline which sometimes prepares the young to die;
which, by sharp trials of anguish, and long days
of weariness, weans them from that keen sense of
mortal enjoyment which is so naturally theirs;
which, through the attenuation of the body, illu-
minates the soul, and, as it steals the bloom from
the cheek, kindles the lustre of faith in the eye,
and makes even that young spirit look, unfaltering, across the dark river, and, putting aside its
earthly loves and its reasonable expectations, exclaim, "Now I am ready!"   But it would
appear that equal preparation, though in different
forms, is provided for most of us, in the various
experiences of sorrow which we are called upon to
know, and which, if we would but heed them,

have a celestial mission, seeking to draw us up from this lower state, to induce us to lay up our treasure where neither moth nor rust corrupts. And in the Christian view of man as an heir of the spiritual word, does not sorrow, in this its *weaning* tendency, receive a most beautiful explanation?

And, because it accomplishes this work, may be the reason why sorrow always wears a kind of *supernatural* character. It is true that blessings, equally with afflictions, come from Heaven; but this truth is not so generally felt. A sharp disappointment will suddenly drive us to God. The mariner of life sails, unthinking, over its prosperous seas, but a flaw of storm will bring him to his prayers. And religion, reason as we will, is peculiarly associated with affliction. And does not sorrow possess this supernatural air, not merely because it interrupts the usual order of things, but because, more than joy, it has a weaning and spiritual tendency, — is sent, as it were, more directly from God for this specific purpose? At least, after the sanctifying experience of sorrow, we hold our joys more religiously.

There are other tendencies of sorrow akin to this, upon which I might dwell, and which show the explanation that it receives in the Christian light. The humbling effect that it has upon the proud and hard-hearted; the *equalizing* result which it works, making the rich and poor, the obscure and the great, stand upon the level of the common humanity, — the common liability and dependence. I might, expanding the topic already touched upon, speak of the influence which sorrow sheds abroad, chastening the light, attempering the draught of joy, and thus keeping our hearts better balanced than otherwise. But I have sufficiently illustrated its mission. I have shown its use, even its beauty, in the Christian view. I have shown why Christianity, as the universal religion, is rightly styled the "religion of sorrow," and why Christ, as the perfect teacher and example, was "a man of sorrows, and acquainted with grief."

Let us all, then, recognize the fact that life itself is a discipline. That for each of us sorrow is mingled with joy in order that this discipline may be accomplished. No one reaches the noon of life without some grief, some disappointment, some sharp trial, which assures him, if he will but heed it, that life is already declining, and that his spirit should train itself for a higher and more permanent state. In the failure of mortal excellence let him recognize the proof of an immortal good, and from the bitterness that mingles with these earthly waters, turn to drink of the celestial fountain. Of all things, let us not receive sorrow indifferently, or without reflection. Its mission is for discipline, but we feel it to be discipline only by recognizing its source and its meaning; "it yieldeth the peaceable fruits of righteousness" only "to them that are *exercised* thereby." Otherwise, it may come and go as the storm that rends the oak, or the drenching tempest that glides off as it falls. It may startle us for a moment, — it may hurt us with a sense of pain and loss, — it may awe us with its mystery; but unless it rouses us to solemn thought upon the meaning of life, to self-communion and prayer, to higher and holier action, it availeth little. It should not smite the heart's chords to wring from them a mere shriek of distress, but to inspire it with a deeper and more elevated tone, and by the element of sadness which it infuses make a more liquid and exquisite melody.

But while we are thus taught to chasten our views of life, and to hold even our joys with seriousness, and with wise forethought, let us not look upon things with any morbid vision, or cast over them a monotonous hue. Let us not live in gloom and bitterness. The Christian, of all others, is the best fitted for a cheerful and proper enjoyment of life, because he wisely recognizes the use of things, understands their evanescent nature, and sees the infinite goodness that has so ordained it. He is not surprised by *sudden* terrors. He is prepared for sorrow, and thus can rest in peace with the good that he has; while those who bury heart and soul in the present enjoyment, and know nothing but sensual good, are broken down by calamity. The sudden change, like a thunder-gust, puts out their light, and darkens all their life; and it is they who are apt to fall from the summit of delight into a morbid gloom; while the Christian, with his balanced soul, inhabits neither extreme.

Finally, let us remember that it is not the object of sorrow to overcome, but to elevate; not to conquer us, but that we, by it, should conquer. It converts the thorns that wound us into a crown. It makes us strong by the baptism of tears. The saint is always a hero. This explains that grand distinction between Heathen and Christian art, of which I spoke in the commencement; that expression of power blended with agony, — of celestial beatitude refining itself upon the face of grief. Christianity has made martyrdom sublime, and sorrow triumphant. Christ is "the Captain of our salvation," — the leader of "many sons unto glory;" for he was "a man of sorrows, and acquainted with grief."

Christian Consolation in Loneliness.

Christian Consolation in Loneliness.

And yet I am not alone, because the Father is with me. JOHN xvi. 32.

THESE words are found in the farewell address of Jesus to his disciples. They were uttered in the dark hour of coming agony, and in the face of an ignominious death. Because Christ was divinely empowered, and possessed the spirit without measure, let us not suppose that to him there was no pain or sorrow, in that great crisis. With all his supernatural dignity, he appears to us far more attractive when we consider him as impressible by circumstances, — as moved by human sympathies. He is thus not merely a teacher, but a pattern for us. In all our trials he not only enables us to endure and to triumph, but draws us close to himself by the affinity of his own experience. We see, too, how the best men, men of the clearest faith, may still look upon death with a shudder, and shrink from the dark and narrow valley; not because they fear death, as such, but because of the agony of dissolution, the rupture of all familiar ties, and the solemn mystery of the last change.

But death and suffering, as Jesus was now to meet them, appeared in no ordinary forms. He was to bear affliction with no friendly consolations around him; but *alone!* — alone in the wrestling of the garden, and amid the cruel mockery. Not upon the peaceful death-bed, but upon the bare and rugged cross, torn by nails, pierced with the spear, crowned with thorns, taunted by the revilings of the multitude, the vinegar and the gall. He must be deserted, and encounter these trials *alone.* He must be rejected, betrayed, crucified *alone.* And as he spoke to his disciples those words of affection and holiness — those words so full of counsel and sublime consolation — he remembered all this; he remembered that they who now clung to him, and listened in sorrow to his parting accents, would soon be scattered as sheep without a shepherd, and leave him to himself in all that shame and agony. But even as he foretold it there gleamed upon his spirit the sunshine of an inner consciousness, — a comfort that no cloud could darken; and instantly he added, "And yet I am not alone, because the Father is with me."

Having thus considered the circumstances in which these words were spoken, I now proceed to draw from them a few reflections.

I would say, then, in the first place, that the great test which proves the excellence of the religion of Christ is its adaptation to man in solitude, — to man as a solitary being; because it is then that he is thrown upon the resources of his own soul, — upon his inner and everlasting life. In society he finds innumerable objects to attract his attention, and to absorb his affections. The ordinary cares of every day, the pursuit of his favorite scheme, the converse of friends, the exciting topics of the season, the hours of recreation, all fill up his time, and occupy his mind with matters external to himself. And looking upon him merely in these relations, if we could forget its great social bearings, and the harmonies which flow from its all-pervading spirit out into every condition of life, we might, perhaps, say that man could get along well enough without religion. If this world were made up merely of business and pleasure, perhaps the atheist's theory would suffice, and we might feel indifferent whether controlled by plastic matter or intelligent mind. We will admit that happiness, in one sense of the term, does not essentially depend upon religion. Nay, we *must* admit this proposition. A man may be happy without being religious. Good health, good spirits; — how many, possessing these, really enjoy life, without being devout, or religious, according to any legitimate meaning of that term.

But change the order of circumstances. Remove these external helps, — substitute therefor sorrow, duty, the revelations of our own inner being, — and all this gayety vanishes like the sparkles from a stream when the storm comes up. The soul that has depended upon outward congenialities for its happiness has no permanent *principle* of happiness; for that is the distinction which religion bestows. He who cannot retire within himself, and find his best resources there, is fitted, perhaps, for the smoother passages of life, but poorly prepared for *all* life. He who cannot and *dare* not turn away from these outward engrossments, and be in spiritual solitude, — who is afraid or sickens at the idea of being alone, — has a brittle possession in all that happiness which comes from the whirl and surface of things. One hour may scatter it forever. And poorly, I repeat, is he prepared for all life, — for some of the most serious and important moments of life. These, as I shall proceed to show, we must meet alone, and from within; and, therefore, it constitutes the blessedness of the Christian religion that it enables man when in solitude to have communion, consolation, and guidance. In fact, it makes him, when alone, to be not alone, — to say, with glad consciousness, "I am not alone, because the Father is with me."

To illustrate this truth, then, I say, that so far as the communion and help of this outward world and of human society are concerned, there are many and important seasons when man must be alone. In the first place, in his most interior and essential nature, man is a solitary being. He is an *individual*, a unit, amid all the souls around him, and all other things, — a being distinct and peculiar as a star. God, in all the variety of his works, has made no man exactly like another. There is an individual isolation, a conscious personality, which he can share with no other; which

resists the idea of absorption; which claims its
own distinct immortality; which has its own
wants and woes, its own sense of duty, its own
spiritual experiences.   Christianity insists upon
nothing more strongly than this.   Piercing below
all conventionalisms, it recognizes man as an individual soul, and, as such, addresses him with its
truths and its sanctions.   Indeed, it bases its
grand doctrine of human brotherhood and equality
upon the essential individuality of each man, because each represents all, — each has in *himself*
the nature of every other.   It demands individual
repentance, individual holiness, individual faith.
One cannot believe for another.   One cannot decide questions of conscience for another.   One
cannot bear the sins or appropriate the virtues
of another.   It is true, we have relations to the
great whole, to the world of mankind, and to the
material universe.   We are linked to these by
subtle affinities.   We are interwoven with them
all, — bound up with them in arterial unity and

life. They have all poured their results into our souls, and helped to form us, and do now support us; and we, in like manner, reäct upon them, and upon others. This truth is a vital one, not to be neglected. But a deeper truth than this, and one upon which this depends, is the individual peculiarity of each, — his integral distinctness, without which there would be no such thing as union, or relationship; nothing but monotony and inertia.

The great fact, then, which I would impress upon you is, that, *essentially*, as spiritual beings, we are *alone*. And I remark that there are experiences in life when we are made to feel this deep fact; when each must deal with his reason, his heart, his conscience, for himself; when each is to act as if sole-existent in the universe, realizing that he is a spirit breathed from God, complete in himself, subject to all spiritual laws, interested in all spiritual welfare; when no stranger soul, though it be that of his dearest friend, can intermeddle with all that occupies him, or share it.

Such experiences we have when reflection binds us to the past.   Memory then opens for us a volume that no eye but God's and ours can read; — memories of neglect, of sin, of deep secrets that our hearts have hidden in their innermost folds. Such experiences sometimes there are when we muse upon the external universe; when we reflect upon the vastness of creation, the littleness of human effort, the transciency of human relations; when our souls are drawn away from all ordinary communions, and we feel that we are drifting before an almighty will, bound to an inevitable destiny, hemmed in by irresistible forces.   Then, with every tie of association shrinking from us; then, keeping the solitary vigil; then, with cold, vast nature all around us, we are *alone*.   Or, there is a solitude which oppresses us even in the heart of the great city; — a solitude more intense even than that of naked nature; when all faces are strange to us; when no pulse of sympathy throbs from our heart to the hearts of others;

9

when each passes us by, engaged with his own destiny, and leaving us to fulfil ours. In this tantalizing solitude of the crowd, in this sense of isolation from our fellows, if never before, do we feel, with sickness of heart, that we are *alone*. There is the solitude of sickness, — the solitude of the watcher or of the patient, — a solitude to which, at times, duty and Providence call us all. There are, in brief, countless circumstances of life when we shall realize that we are indeed alone; and sad enough will be that solitude if we have no inner resource, — no Celestial companionship; — if we cannot say, and feel as we say it, that we are not alone, for the Father is with us.

But, while I cannot specify all these forms of solitude, let me dwell upon two or three of the experiences of life in which we are peculiarly alone.

First, then, I would say, that we must be alone in the *pursuit of Truth* and *the work of Duty*. Others may aid me in these, but I must decide

and act for myself. I must believe for myself.
I must do right for myself; or if I do wrong, it
is also for myself, and in myself I realize the ret-
ribution. By my own sense of right and wrong
— by my own standard of truth and falsehood —
I must stand or fall. There is in this world
nothing so great and solemn as the struggles of
the solitary soul in its researches after the truth,
— in its endeavors to obey the right. We may
be indifferent to these vital questions, — it is to be
feared that many are; we may glide along in the
suppleness of habit, and the ease of conventional-
ism; we may never trouble ourselves with any
pungent scruples; we may never pursue the task
of introspection, or bring to bear upon the fibres
of motive and desire within us the intense focus of
God's moral law; we may never vex our souls
with tests of faith, but rest contented with the
common or hereditary standard; — but he who
will be serious in the work of spiritual discipline,
who will act from a vital law of duty, must endure

struggles and conflicts than which, I repeat, there is nothing more solemn under the sun. He will often find himself opposed to the general current of human faith and action. His position will be singular. His principle will be tried. Interest will direct him another way; his strictness will be ridiculed, his motives questioned, his sincerity misunderstood and aspersed. Alone must he endure all this, — alone cling to the majestic ideal of right as it rises to his own soul. And thus he must wage a bitter conflict with fear and with seduction, — with sophistries of the heart, and reluctance of the will.

Often, too, must he question his own motives with a severer judgment than that of the world, as his scrutiny is more close, and his self-knowledge more minute. He knows the secret sin, the mental act, the spiritual aberration. He knows the distance between his highest effort and that lofty standard of perfection to which he has pledged his purposes. Alone, alone does the great conflict go on within him. The struggle, the self-denial, the pain, and the victory, are of the very essence of martyrdom, — are the chief peculiarities in the martyr's lot. His, too, must be the solitude of prayer, when, throwing by all entanglements, — in his naked individuality, — he wrestles at the Mercy Seat, or soars to the bliss of Divine communion. In such hours, — in every hour of self-communion, — when we ask ourselves the highest questions respecting faith and duty, it is the deepest comfort to the religious soul to feel and to say, "I am not alone, for the Father is with me."

Again; there are experiences of *Sorrow* in which we are peculiarly alone. How often does the soul feel this when it is suffering from the loss of friends! Then we find no comfort in external things. Pleasure charms not; business cannot cheat us of our grief; wealth supplies not the void; and though the voice of friendship falls in consolation upon the ear, yet, with all these, we are alone, — *alone!* No other spirit can fully comprehend our woe, or enter into our desolation. No human eye can pierce to our sorrows; no sympathy can share them. Alone we must realize their sharp suggestions, their painful memories, their brood of sad and solemn thoughts. The mother bending over her dead child; — O! what solitude is like that? — where such absolute loneliness as that which possesses her soul, when she takes the final look of that little pale face crowned with flowers and sleeping in its last chamber, with the silent voice of the dead uttering its last *good night?* What more solitary than the spirit of one who, like the widow of Nain, follows to the grave her only son? — of one from whom the wife, the mother, has been taken? The mourner is in solitude, — alone, in this peopled world; — O, how utterly alone! Through the silent valley of tears wanders that stricken spirit, seeing only memorials of its loss.

Indeed, sorrow of any kind is solitary. Its

deepest pangs, its most solemn visitations, are in the secrecy of the individual soul. We labor to conceal it from others. We wear a face of unconcern or gayety amid the multitude. Society is thronged with masked faces. Unseen burdens of woe are carried about in its busy haunts. The man of firm step in the mart, and of vigorous arm in the workshop, has communions in his chamber that make him weak as a child. Nothing is more deceitful than a happy countenance. Haggard spirits laugh over the wine-cup, and the blooming garland of pleasure crowns an aching head. For sorrow is secret and solitary. Each "heart knoweth its own bitterness."

How precious, then, in the loneliness of sorrow, is that faith which bids us look up and see how near is God, and feel what divine companionship is ours, and know what infinite sympathy engirds us, — what concern for our good is, even in this darkness, shaping out blessings for us, and distilling from this secret agony everlasting peace for the soul. How precious that faith in the clear vision of which we can say, " I am not alone, for the Father is with me."

Finally, we must experience *Death* alone. As I said in the commencement, the best, the most pious soul, may naturally shrink from this great event. We may learn to anticipate it with resignation, to look upon it with trust; but indifference respecting it is no proof of religion. It would be, rather, a bad sign for one to approach it without emotion; for however his faith may penetrate beyond, the religious spirit will, with deep awe, lift that curtain of mystery which hangs before the untried future. That is a fact which we must encounter alone. Friends may gather around us; their ministrations may aid, their consolations soothe us. They may be with us to the very last; they may cling to us as though they would pluck us back to the shores of time; their voices may fall, the last of earthly sounds, upon our ears; their kiss awaken the last throb of consciousness; but they cannot go with us, they cannot die in our stead; the last time must come, — they must loosen their hold from us, and fade from our vision, and we become wrapt in the solemn experience of death, *alone!* Alone must we tread the dark valley, — alone embark for the unseen land. No, Christian! *not* alone. To your soul, thus separated in blank amazement from all familiar things, still is that vision of faith granted that so often lighted your earthly perplexities; to you is it given, in this most solitary hour, to say, " I am not alone, for the Father is with me ! "

I repeat, then, in closing, that the test which proves the excellence of the religion of Christ is the fact that it fits us for those solemn hours of life when we must be alone. Mere happiness we may derive from other sources; but *this* consolation not all the world can give, — the world cannot take it away.

Let us remember, then, that though we seldom look within — though our affections may be absorbed in external things — these solitary seasons will come. It behoves us, therefore, as we value true peace of mind, genuine happiness, which connects us to the throne of God with golden links of prayer, — it behoves each to ask himself, "Dare I be alone? Am I ready to be alone? And what report will my soul make in that hour of solitude? If I do wrong, if I cleave to the evil rather than the good, what shall I do when I am alone, and yet not alone, but with the Father? But if I do right, if I trust in Him, and daily walk with Him, what crown of human honor. what store of wealth, what residuum of earthly pleasure, can compare with the glad consciousness that wherever I rest or wander, in every season and circumstance, in the solitary hours of life, and the loneliness of death, God is verily with me?

Surely, no attainment is equal to that strength of Christ, by which, when approaching the cross, he was able to say, "I am not alone, for the Father is with me." By this strength, he was able to do more than to say and feel thus. He was able to strengthen others, — to exclaim, " Be of good cheer, I have overcome the world." So we, by spiritual discipline, having learned of Christ to be thus strong, not only possess a spring of unfailing consolation for ourselves, but there shall go out from us a benediction and a power that shall gladden the weary and fortify the weak, — that shall fill the solitude of many a lonely spirit with the consolations of the Father's love, and the bliss of the Father's presence.

Resignation.

Resignation.

The cup which my Father hath given me, shall I not drink it? JOHN xviii. 11.

THE circumstances in which these words were uttered have, doubtless, often arrested your attention, — have often been delineated for you by others. Yet it is always profitable for us to recur to them They transpired immediately after our Saviour's farewell with his disciples. The entire transaction in that "upper room" had been hallowed and softened by the fact of his coming death. He saw that fact distinctly before him, and to his eye everything was associated with it. As he took the bread and broke it, it seemed to him an emblem of himself, pierced and dying; and from the fulness of his spirit he spoke, " Take, eat, this is my *body*, broken for you." As he took the cup and set it before them, it reminded him of his *blood*, that must flow ere his mission was fulfilled, and he could say, " It is finished." And then, when the traitor rose from that table to go out and consummate the very purpose that should lead to that event, as one who had arrayed himself in robes of death, and was about to declare his legacy, he broke forth in that subline strain commencing, " Now is the Son of man glorified, and God is glorified in him;" — that strain of mingled precept, and promise, and warning, and prayer, from which the weary and the sick-hearted of all ages shall gather strength and consolation, and which shall be read in dying chambers and houses of mourning until death and sorrow shall reign no more.

Laden, then, with the thought of his death, he had gone with his disciples into the garden of Gethsemane. There, in the darkness and loneliness of night, the full anguish of his situation rushed upon his spirit. He shrank from the rude scenes that opened before him,—from the mocker's sneer and the ruler's scourge; from the glare of impatient revenge, and the weeping eyes of helpless friendship; from the insignia of imposture and of shame; and from the protracted, thirsty, torturing death. He shrank from these, — he shrank from the rupture of tender ties, — he shrank from the parting with deeply-loved friends, — his soul was overburdened, his spirit was swollen to agony, and he rushed to his knees, and prayed, "Father, if thou be willing, remove this cup from me." Yet even then, in the intensity of his grief, the sentiment that lay deep and serene below suggested the conditions, and he added, "Nevertheless, not my will, but thine, be done." But still the painful thought oppressed him, and, though more subdued now, he knelt and prayed again, "O, my Father, if this cup may not pass away from me except I drink it, thy will be done." And once more, as he returned from his weary, sleeping disciples,

10

and found himself alone, the wish broke forth
— yet tempered by the same obedient com-
pliance.

And here I pause to ask, if, in all that scene of
agony, anything is developed inconsistent with the
character of Christ? If we would have it otherwise? If these tears and groans of anguish are
tokens of a weakness that we would conceal from
our convictions, — that we would overlook, as
marring the dignity and the divinity of the Saviour? For one, I would not have it otherwise.
I would not have the consoling strength, the
sympathizing tenderness, the holy victory that
may be drawn from thence, — I would not have
these left out from the Life that was given us as a
pattern. Jesus, we are told, "was made perfect
through suffering." This struggle took place that
victory might be won; — this discipline of sorrow
fell upon him that perfection and beauty might
be developed. By this we see that Christ's was
a spirit liable to trial, — impressible by suffering;

and from this fact does the victory appear greater and more real. In this we see one striving with man's sorrow, — seeking, like man, to be delivered from pain and grief, yet rising to a calm obedience, — a lofty resignation. Had Jesus passed through life always serene, always un- shrinking, we should not have seen a man, but something that man is not, something that man cannot be in this world; and that calm question, "The cup that my Father hath given me, shall I not drink it?" would lose its force and significance. Otherwise, why should not Jesus be as resigned then as before? He had betrayed no sense of suffering, no impressibility by pain; why should he not be willing, seeing he was always able to meet the end? But O! when the resignation has been born in wrestling and in prayer, — when that deep, holy calmness has fallen upon a soul that has been tossed by sorrow, and that has shrunk from death, — when the brow has come up smooth and radiant from the shadow of mourning, — when that soul is ready for the issue, not because it has always felt around it the girdle of Omnipotence, but because, through weakness and suffering, it has risen and worked out an unfaltering trust, and taken hold of the hand of God by the effort of faith, — then it is, I say, that resignation is beautiful and holy, — then do we wonder and admire.

So was it with Jesus. A little while ago we saw him bowed with sorrow, his eyes lifted with tears to heaven. We saw that he keenly felt the approaching pain, and shame, and death. A little while ago, the still night air was laden with his cry, "Father, if it be thy will, let this cup pass from me." And now, as one who is strong and ready, he says calmly to Peter, "The cup which my Father hath given me, shall I not drink it?" Truly, a battle has been fought, and a victory won, here; but we should not be the better for it, were it not for that very process of suffering in which that battle was waged, and from which that victory was wrung. Now, when *we* sorrow, we know who also sorrowed; we remember whose agony the still heavens looked upon with all their starry eyes, — whose tears moistened the bosom of the bare earth, — whose cry of anguish pierced the gloom of night. Now, too, when we sorrow, we know where to find relief; we learn that spirit of resignation, and under what conditions it may be born. Thank God, then, for the lesson of the lonely garden and the weeping Christ — *we*, too, may be "made perfect through suffering."

Such, then, were the circumstances that illustrate the words of the text. Scarcely had Jesus risen from his knees, and wakened the drowsy disciples, when the light of lanterns flashed upon him, and Judas came with a multitude to bear him to that death from which, but now, he shrunk with agony. But he shrunk no more. The trial was over, — the darkness had vanished, — an angel had strengthened him; and when the impetuous

Peter drew his sword and smote off the servant's ear, his master turned to him, with the calm rebuke, " Put up thy sword into his sheath; the cup which my Father hath given me, shall I not drink it?" Yes, cold and bitter as that cup was, pressed now to his very lips, he had learned to drink it; God had given him strength, and no more did he falter, no more did he groan — save once, for a moment, when, upon the cross, drooping, and racked with intense pain, he cried out, "My God, my God, why hast thou forsaken me?" But that passed away in the triumphant ejaculation, " It is finished ! "

Such was the resignation of Jesus; a trait in his character which, like all the rest, is not only to be admired, but imitated; — not an abstract virtue, manifested by a being so perfect and so enshrined in the sanctity of a divine nature that we cannot approach it, and in our mortal, work-day trials can never feel it; but a virtue which should be throned in every heart, the strength and consolation of which every suffering soul may experience. Nay, if there is one virtue which is more often needed than any other, which lies at the base of true happiness, and than which there is no surer seal of piety, it is this virtue of resignation. And let me proceed to say, that by resignation I mean not cold and sullen apathy, or reckless hardihood, but a sweet trust and humble acquiescence, which show that the soul has submitted itself to the Father who knows and does best, and that it meets his dispensations with obedience and his mysteries with faith. The apathy and hardihood to which I have alluded are very far from the trust and piety of a religious spirit. The fatalist acquiesces in the course of things because he cannot help it. He has reasoned to the conclusion that his murmuring and weeping will not alter matters, and he has resolved to take things as they come. But here is no resignation to the will of God, but to the necessity of things. Here is no faith that all things are wisely ordered, and that sorrow is but the shadow of the Father's hand. No; here is the simple belief that things are as they are, and cannot be altered, — that an arbitrary law is the eternal rule, not a benevolent and holy purpose; and the philosopher would be just as resigned if he believed all things to be under the guidance of a blind fate, whose iron machinery drives on to level or exalt, unintelligent and remorseless, whether in its course it brings about good or evil, — whether it gladdens human hearts or crushes them. Such resignation as this may be quite common in the world, manifested in various phases, and by men of different religious opinions. Do we not often hear the expression, " Well, things are as they are, — we do best to take them as they come;" and here the matter ends? No higher reference is made. The things alluded to may issue from the bosom of material nature, may be sent into the world by chance, or may come from the good Father of all; but the minds of these reasoners reach not so far. Now

I repeat, there is no religion and no true philosophy in this method; certainly it is not such resignation as Jesus manifested. In fact, it indicates total carelessness as to the discipline of life, and will generally be found with men in whose thoughts God is not, or to whose conceptions he is the distant, inactive Deity, not the near and ever-working Controller. I cannot admire the conduct of that man who when the bolt of sorrow falls, receives it upon the armor of a rigid fatalism, who wipes scarcely a tear from his hard, dry face, and says, " Well, it cannot be helped; things are so ordered." Below all this there is often a sulky, half-angry sentiment, as though the victim felt the blow, but was determined not to wince, — as though there was an acknowledgment of weakness, but also a display of pride, — a feeling that we cannot resist sorrow, yet that sorrow has no business to come, and now that it has come the sufferer will not yield to it. This, evidently, is not resignation, religious resignation, but only sullen acquiescence, or reckless hardihood.

In a certain sense it is true that we do well to take things as they come, — that we cannot help the eternal laws that control events. But we must go behind this truth. Whence do events come, and for what purpose do they come? What is life, and for what end are all its varied dispensations? Religion points us up beyond the cloud of materialism, and behind the mechanism of nature, to an Infinite Spirit, to a God, to a Father. All things are moved by infinite Love. Life is not merely a phenomenon, it is a *Lesson*. Its events do not come and go, in a causeless, arbitrary manner; they are meant for our discipline and our good. In whatever aspect they come, then, let their appropriate lesson be heeded. This is the religious view of life, and is wide apart from the philosophy that lets events happen as they will, as though we were in the setting of a heady current, and were borne along among other matters that now help us, now jar and wound us, — that happen without order and without object; all, like ourselves, driven along and taking things as they come. In the religious view, all things stream from God's throne, and whatever sky hangs over them, the infinite One is present; prosperity is the sunshine that he has sent, and Faith, as she weeps, beholds a bow in the clouds.

The religious man takes things as they come, but how? In a reverent and filial spirit, a spirit that obeys and trusts because God has ordained. He refers, behind the event, to the will that declares it. And yet, this will be no formal, lifeless resignation. He will not be stripped of his manhood, or become unnatural in his religion. His resignation will not be the cold assent of reason, or the mere rote and repetition of the lips. No, it will be born in struggling and in sorrow. Religion is not a process that makes our nature callous to all fierce heats or drenching storms. Neither is he the most religious man who is calmest in the keen crisis of trouble. I say in the *crisis* of trouble — for to human vision there always is a crisis. We cannot penetrate to the secret determinations of God, and in the season of care and affliction there is a time when the issue is uncertain, — when we cannot say it is sealed. What shall we do then? Is human agency nothing? Grant that we *are* driving down a stream, — can we use no effort? Is there not a time when deeds, struggles, prayers, are of some avail? — when the spirit, in its intense agony, with swollen strength and surging tears, heaves against the catastrophe, if yet, perchance, it may ward it off? Truely, there is such a time, and the humblest disciple of Christ may weep as he also wept. But let him also strive as Christ strove. Let him not dash his grief in rebellious billows to the throne; let not his groans arise in resentful murmurs; let the remembrance of what God is and why he does, be with him, and let the filial, reverent trust steal in, — " Not my will, but thine be

done." That reference to God, that obedience to
him, rising from the very depths of sorrow, and
clung to without faltering, is RESIGNATION. It
shall bestow peace and victory in the end. O!
how different from that sullen fatalism that lets
things come as they will. To such a soul things
do come as they will, and it hardens under them,
— they *do* come as they will, but it sees not, cares
not, why they come. No thought goes up beyond
the cloud to God, — no strength is born that shall
make life's trials lighter, — no love and faith that
will seek the Father's hand in the darkest hour,
and shed an enduring light over the thorny path
of affliction, and upon the bosom of the grave.
Look at these two. Outwardly, their calmness
may be the same. Nay, the one may evince
emotion and tears, while the other shall stand rigid
in the hour of calamity, with a bitter smile, or a
frown of endurance. But in the one is strength,
in the other rigidity; in the one is power to
triumph over sorrow, in the other only nervous

capacity to resist it. The one is man hardened to indifference, sullen because of irreligion, upon whom some sorrow will one day fall that will peel him to the quick, and he will not know where to flee for healing. The other is man contending against evil, yet not against God, — man with all the tenderness and strength of his nature, impressible yet unconquerable, walking with feet that bleed among the wounding thorns, and a heart that shrinks from the heavy woe, yet, all lacerated as he is, able to walk through, because he holds by the hand of Omnipotence. The one is the unbending tree, peeled by the lightning and stripped by the north wind, lifting its gnarled head in sullen defiance to the storm, which, when the storm does overcome it, shall be broken. The other also is rooted in strength, and meets the rushing blast with a lofty front. But as "it smiles in sunshine, so it bends in storm," trustful and obedient, yet firm and brave, and nothing shall overwhelm it.

I trust I have succeeded in impressing upon you

the difference between Christian resignation and mere hardihood, or indifference. Resignation is born of discipline, and lives only in a truly religious soul. We have seen that it is not incompatible with tenderness; nay, it is more valuable, because it springs up in natures that have thus suffered and wept. To see *them* become calm and strong, and pass with unfaltering step through the valley of affliction, when, but now, they shrunk from it, is a proof that God indeed has strengthened them, and that they have had communion with him. The unbeliever's stubbornness may endure to the end, but no human power could inspire this sudden and triumphant calmness.

And even when the crisis is past, when the sorrow is sealed, it is not rebellion to sigh and weep. Our Father has made us so. He has opened the springs of love that well up within us, and can we help mourning when they turn to tears and blood? He has made very tender the ties that bind us to happiness, and can we fail to

shrink and suffer when they are cut asunder?
When we have labored long in the light of hope,
and lo! it goes out in darkness, and the blast of
disappointment rushes upon us, can we help being
sad? Can the mother prevent weeping when she
kisses the lips of her infant that shall prattle to
her no more; when she presses its tiny hand, so
cold and still, — the little hand that has rested
upon her bosom, and twined in her hair; and even
when it is so sweet and beautiful that she could
strain it to her heart forever, it is laid away in the
envious concealment of the grave? Can the wife,
or the husband, help mourning, when the partner
and counsellor is gone, — when home is made very
desolate because the familiar voice sounds not
there, and the cast-off garment of the departed is
strangely vacant, and the familiar face has vanished, never more to return? Can the child fail
to lament, when the father, the mother, — the
being who nurtured him in infancy, who pillowed
his head in sickness, who prayed for him with

tears in his sinful wandering, who ever rejoiced
in his joy and wept in his sorrows, — can he
fail to weep when that venerable form lies all
enshrouded, and the door closes upon it, and the
homestead is vacant, and the link that bound him
to childhood is in the grave? Say, can we check
the gush of sorrow at any of life's sharp trials
and losses? No; nor are we forbidden to weep,
nor would we be human if we did not weep, — if,
at least, the spirit did not quiver when the keen
scathing goes over it. But *how* shall we weep?
O! Thou, who didst suffer in Gethsemane, thou
hast taught us how. By thy sacred sorrow and
thy pious obedience thou hast taught us; by thy
great agony and thy sublime victory thou hast
taught us. We must refer all to God. We must
earnestly, sincerely say, "Thy will be done."
Then our prayers will be the source of our
strength. Then our sorrowing will bring us comfort. "Thy will be done;" repeat this, feel this,
realize its meaning and its relations, and you shall

11

be able to say, with a rooted calmness, "The cup which my Father hath given me, shall I not drink it?"

"The cup which my Father hath given me, shall I not drink it?" Who shall be able to say this as Jesues said it? They who struggle as he struggled, — who obey as he obeyed, — who trust as he trusted. There are those upon earth who have been able to say it. It has made them stronger and happier. There are those in heaven who have been able to say it They have gone up from earthly communions to the communion on high. Do you not see them there, walking so serenely by the still waters, with palms about their brows? Serenely — for in their faces nothing is left of their conflict but its triumph; nothing of their swollen agony but the massy, enduring strength it has imparted. They have ceased from their trials, but first they learned how to endure them. They submitted, but they were not overwhelmed. When sorrow came, each pious soul struggled, but trusted; and so it was able to meet the last struggle. — was able to say, as the shadow of death fell upon it, "The cup which my Father hath given me, shall I not drink it?" They were resigned. Behold — theirs is the victory!

The Mission of Little Children.

The Mission of Little Children.

And Jesus called a little child unto him, and set him in the midst of them. MATTHEW xviii. 2.

EVERYTHING has its mission. I speak not now of the office which each part of the great universe discharges. I speak not of the relation between these parts, — that beautiful ordinance by which the whole is linked together in one common life, by which the greatest is dependent upon the least, and the least shares in the benefactions of the greatest. In this sense, everything has, strictly, its mission. But I speak of the influence, the instruction, which everything has, or may have, for the soul of man. The flower, and the star, the grass of the field, the outspread ocean, are full of lessons; they perform

a mission to our spiritual nature, if we will receive it. We may pass them by as simply material
forms, the decorations or conveniencies of this
our sensual life. But if we will come to them in
a religious spirit, and study all their meaning, they
will be to us ministers of God, impressive and
eloquent as human lips, and filled with truths in-
structive as any that man can utter.

Jesus illustrated his teachings by these objects.
He made everything that was at hand perform a
mission for the human soul. The lilies of the
field were clothed with spiritual suggestion, and
the fowls of the air, as they flew through the
trackless firmament, bore a lesson of truth and
consolation. As if to show that there is nothing,
however small, that is insignificant, and that has
not its mission, he selected the falling sparrow to
be a minister of wisdom, and dignified the way-
side well as a clear and living oracle of the di-
vinest truth.

In the instance before us, the object selected

was a little child. In reply to the question, "Who is the greatest in the kingdom of heaven?" Jesus set this little one in the midst of his disciples, and said, " Verily I say unto you, except ye be converted, and become as little children, ye shall not enter into the kingdom of heaven." Thus did he rebuke their sensuous ideas of greatness by a spiritual truth, and make a little child the teacher of profound and beautiful wisdom. I do not propose, however, at this time, to dwell upon the precise doctrines which Christ taught in this instance, but having, as it were, the little child set in our midst, to draw from it further lessons that may do us good. In one word, I propose to speak of *the mission of little children.*

In using this term "*mission*," I wish to have no obscurity about my meaning. I refer, by it, to the influence which little children may exert upon us, — to the effects which they may produce, — rather than to any direct object which they can have in view, or for which they set themselves to work. They may be unconscious missionaries; indeed, to a great extent, they are so. But so are the lilies of the field and the birds of the air. Yet if we believe that God is the ordainer of all wisdom and of all good, that he uses an object or event in numberless ways, and makes it the unconscious instrument of many of his plans, then we may say that children are *sent* by him for the express purpose of producing these effects, and in that sense have a mission.

I pass to consider some of the modes in which that mission is accomplished.

I. Little children give us *a sincere and af-fectionate manifestation of human nature.* I know that even a child will soon become artful, and imbibe the spirit of dealing and of policy. But, in a strongly comparative sense, the child is artless. The thoughts of the heart leap spontane-ously from the lips. The bubbling impulse is closely followed by the action. Its desire, its aversion, its love, its curiosity, are expressed without modification. That broken prattle, those half-pronounced words, are uttered with clear, ringing tones of sincerity. There is no coil of deceit about the heart. There are no secrets chambered in the brain. The countenance has put on no disguise. There is no manœuvring with lips or actions, no suspicion or plotting in the eyes. It is simple human nature fresh from the hands of God, with all its young springs in motion, trying themselves in their simplicity and their newness. The eyes open upon the world, not with speculation, but with wonder. To them, the ancient hills and the morning stars are just created, new phenomena burst upon them every moment, and nature in a thousand channels pours itself into the young soul. And how soon it learns the meaning of a mother's smile, and the protection of a father's hand! How soon the fountains of affection are unsealed, and the mystery of human love takes possession of its heart! But the tides of that love are controlled by no calculation, are fettered by no proprieties, but flow artlessly and freely.

Humanity soon runs into deceit, and the sincerest man wears a mask. We cannot trust our most familiar friends, to the whole extent. We all retain something in our inmost hearts that nobody knows but we and God. The world bids us be shrewd and politic. We walk in a mart of selfishness. Eyes stare upon us, and we are afraid of them. We meet as traders, as partisans, as citizens, as worshippers, as friends — brothers, if you will — but we must not surrender too much confidence, we must not express all we think, we must school ourselves in some respects, — must adopt some conventionalities. There is some degree of isolation between ourselves and every other one. But from the world's strife and sordidness, its wearisome forms and cold suspicions, we may turn to the sanctity of home, and, if we have a child there, we shall find affection without alloy, a welcome that leaps from the heart in sunshine to the face, and speaks right from the soul; — a companion who is not afraid or ashamed of us, who makes no calculation about our friendship, who has faith in it, and requires of us perfect faith in return, and whose sincerity rebukes our worldliness, and makes us wonder at the world. And if all this makes us better and happier, if it keeps our hearts from hardness and attrition, if it begets in us something of the same sincerity, and hallows us with something of the same affection, if it softens and purifies us at all, then do not children, in this respect perform a mission for us?

And shall we not learn from them more confidence in human nature, seeing that " the child is father to the man," and that much that seems cold and hard in men may conceal the remains of childhood's better feeling? And, also, shall it not make us deplore and guard against those influences which can change the sincere and loving child into the deceitful and selfish man — that cover the spring of genuine feeling with the thick rime of worldliness, and petrify the tender chords of the heart into rough, unfeeling sinews? The man should not be, in all respects, *as* the child. The child cannot have the glory of the man. If it is not polluted by his vices, it is not ennobled by his virtues. But in so much as the child awakens in us tenderness, and teaches us sincerity, and counteracts our coarser and harder tendencies, and cheers us in our isolation from human hearts, by binding us close with a warm affection, and sheds ever around our path the mirrored sunshine of our youth and our simplicity, in so much the child accomplishes for us a blessed mission.

II. Children teach us *faith* and *confidence.* Man soon becomes proud with reason, and impatient of restraint. He thinks he knows, or ought to know, the whole mystery of the universe. It is not easy for him to take anything upon trust, or to lie low in the hand of God. But the child is full of faith.   He is not old enough to speculate, and the things he sees are to him so strange and wonderful that he can easily believe in "the things that are unseen."   He propounds many questions, but entertains no doubts as to God and heaven. And what confidence has he in his father's government and his mother's providence !

I do not say, here, that a man's faith should be as a child's faith.   Man *must* examine and reason, contend with doubt, and wander through mystery.   But I would have him cherish the feeling that *he* too is a child, the denizen of a Father's house, and have sufficient confidence in that Father to trust his goodness; and to remember, if things look perplexed and discordant to him, that his vision is but a child's vision — he cannot see all.   Indeed, there is a beautiful analogy between a child in its father's house and man in the universe, and much there is in the filial sentiment that belongs to both conditions.   Beautifully has it been shown by a recent writer how the natural operation of this sentiment in the child's heart, and in the sphere of home, stands somewhat in the place of that religion which man needs in his maturer conditions. "God has given it, in its very lot," says he, "a religion of its own, the sufficiency of which it were impiety to doubt. The child's veneration can scarcely climb to any loftier height than the soul of a wise and good parent. . . . . . How can there be for him diviner truth than his father's knowledge, a more wondrous world than his father's experience, a better providence than his mother's vigilance, a securer fidelity than in their united promise? Encompassed round by these, he rests as in the embrace of the only omniscience he can comprehend." *

But O! my friends, when our childhood has passed by, and we go out to drink the mingled cup of life, and cares come crowding upon us, and hopes are crushed, and doubts wrestle with us, and

* Martineau.

sorrow burdens our spirits, then we need a deeper
faith, and look up for a stronger Father. A kind
word will not stifle our grief then. We cannot
go to sleep upon our mother's arms, and forget it
all. There is no charm to hold our spirits within
the walls of this home, the earth. Our thoughts
crave more than this. Our souls reach out over
the grave, and cry for something after! No
bauble will assuage this bitterness. It is spiritual
and stern, and we must have a word from heaven
— a promise from one who is able to fulfill. We
look around us, and find that Father, and his very
nature contains the promise that we need. And
as the child in his ignorance has faith, not because
he can *demonstrate*, but because it is his father,
so let us, in our ignorance, feel that in this great
universe of many mansions, of solemn mysteries, of
homes beyond the earth, of relationships that reach
through eternity, of plans only a portion of which
is seen here; so let us look up as to a Father's
face, take hold of his hand, go in and out and lie

12

down securely in his presence, and cherish *faith*. If children only teach us to do this, how beautiful and how great is their mission!

III. *Children awaken in us new and powerful affections.* Nobody but a parent can realize what these affections are, can tell what a fountain of emotion the newborn child unseals, what chords of strange love are drawn out from the heart, that before lay there concealed. One may have all powers of intellect, a refined moral culture, a noble and wide-reaching philanthropy, and yet a child born to him shall awaken within him a depth of tenderness, a sentiment of love, a yearning affection, that shall surprise him as to the capacity and the mystery of his nature.

And the relation of a mother to her child; what other is like it? Without it, how undeveloped is the great element of affection, how small a horn of its orb is filled and lighted! What was she until that new love woke up within her, and her heart and soul thrilled with it, and first truely lived in it? Of all the degrees of human love, how amply is this the highest! In all the depths of human love, how surely is this the nethermost! When illustrations fail us, how confidently do we seize upon this! The mother nurturing her child in tenderness, watching over it with untiring love! O! *that* is affection stronger than any of this earth. It has a power, a beauty, a holiness, like no other human sentiment. When that child has grown to maturity, and has gone out from her in profligacy and in scorn; when the world has denounced him, and justice sets its price upon his head, and lovers and companions fall off from him in utter loathing — we do not ask, we *know*, there is one heart that cannot reject him. No sin of his can paralyze the chord that vibrates there for him. No alienation can cancel the affection that was born at his birth, that pillowed him in his infancy, centred in him its life, clasped him with its strength, and shed upon him its blessings, its hopes, and its prayers.

And no one feels the death of a child as a mother feels it. Even the father cannot realize it thus. There is a vacancy in his home, and a heaviness in his heart. There is a chain of association that at set times comes round with its broken link; there are memories of endearment, a keen sense of loss, a weeping over crushed hopes, and a pain of wounded affection. But the mother feels that one has been taken away who was still closer to her heart. Hers has been the office of constant ministration. Every gradation of feature has developed before her eyes. She has detected every new gleam of intelligence. She heard the first utterance of every new word. She has been the refuge of his fears; the supply of his wants. And every task of affection has woven a new link, and made dear to her its object. And when he dies, a portion of her own life, as it were, dies. How can she give him up, with all these memories, these associations? The timid hands that have so often taken hers in trust and love, how can she fold them on his breast, and surrender them to the cold clasp of death? The feet whose wanderings she has watched so narrowly, how can she see them straitened to go down into the dark valley? The head that she has pressed to her lips and her bosom, that she has watched in burning sickness and in peaceful slumber, a hair of which she could not see harmed, O! how can she consign it to the chamber of the grave? The form that not for one night has been beyond her vision or her knowledge, how can she put it away for the long night of the sepulchre, to see it here no more? Man has cares and toils that draw away his thoughts and employ them; she sits in loneliness, and all these memories, all these suggestions, crowd upon her. How can she bear all this? She could not, were it not that her faith is as her affection; and if the one is more deep and tender than in man, the other is more simple and spontaneous, and takes confidently hold of the hand of God.

Thus, then, do children awaken within us deep and mighty affections; and is it not their mission to do so? Do we not see many beautiful offices created and discharged by these affections—tender and far-reaching relationships into which they run? Do we not see how they win the heart from frivolity and selfishness, and make it aware of duties, and quick with sympathies? I shall not enter into detailed considerations of the results of this affection thus awakened in us by children. A little reflection will render them obvious to you. Let me simply say, that in awakening these affections children discharge an important and beautiful mission.

IV. I might speak of other offices discharged by little children; of the influence upon us of their purity and their innocence; their importance in the social state; of the benefits conferred upon us by the very duties which we exercise toward them. But merely suggesting these, I will speak at this time of but one more mission which they perform for us. And this, my friends, is performed through sadness and through tears. The little child performs it by its *death*. It has been with us a little while. We have enjoyed its bright and innocent companionship by the dusty highway of life, in the midst of its toils, its cares, and its sin. It has been a gleam of sunshine and a voice of perpetual gladness in our homes. We have learned from it blessed lessons of simplicity, sincerity, purity, faith. It has unsealed within us this gushing, never-ebbing tide of affection. Suddenly, it is taken away. We miss the gleam of sunshine. We miss the voice of gladness. Our homes are dark and silent. We ask, "Shall it not come again?" And the answer breaks upon us through the cold, gray silence, *"Nevermore!"* We say to ourselves again and again, "Can it be possible?" "Do we not dream?" "Will not that life and affection return to us?" *"Nevermore!"* O! nevermore! The heart is like an empty mansion, and that word goes echoing through its desolate chambers. We are stricken and afflicted. But must this, should this, be always and only so? Are we not looking merely at the *earthly* aspect of the event? Has it not a *spiritual* phase for us? Nay, do we not begin to consider how through our temporal affection an eternal good is wrought out for us? Do we not begin to realize that in our souls we have derived profit from it already? Do we not begin to learn that life is not a holiday or a workday only, but a *discipline*, — that God conducts that discipline in infinite wisdom and benevolence, — mingles the draught, and, when he sees fit, infuses bitterness? Not that constant sweet would not please us better, but that our *discipline*, which is of more importance than our indulgence, will be more effectual thereby. This is often talked about; I ask, do not we who are called upon to mourn the loss of children realize it, — actually *realize* that that loss is for our spiritual gain? If we do not, we are merely looking upon the earthly phase of our loss. If we do not realize this spiritual good, we may.

Yes, in death the little child has a mission for us. Through that very departure he accomplishes for us, perhaps, what he could not accomplish by his life. These affections which he has awakened, we have considered how strong they are. They are stronger, are they not, than any attachment to mere things of this earth? But that child has gone from us, — gone into the unseen, the spiritual world. What then? Do our affections sink back into our hearts, — become absorbed and forgotten? O, no! They reach out after that little one; they follow him into the unseen and spiritual world. Thus are we brought in contact with that world, — thus is it made a great and vivid reality to us, — perhaps for the first time. We have talked of it, we have believed in it; but now that our dead have gone into it, we have, as it were, entered it ourselves.

Its atmosphere is around us, chords of affection draw us toward it, the faces of our departed ones look out from it — and it is a reality. And is it not worth something to make it such a reality?

We are wedded to this world. It is beautiful, it is attractive, it is *real*. Immortality is a pleasant thought. The spiritual land is an object of faith. But the separation between this and that is cold to think of, and hard to bear. It needs something stronger than this earth to draw us toward that spiritual world ; to break some of the thousand tendrils that bind us here. My friends, though many powerful appeals, many solid arguments, cannot break our affections from this earth, the hand of a departed child can do it. The voice that calls us to unseen realities, that bids us prepare for the heavenly land, that says from heights of spiritual bliss and purity, " Come up hither ;" — that voice is the voice that we loved so on earth, and gladly can we rise and follow it.

Behold, then, what a little child can perform for us through its death! It makes real and attractive to us that spiritual world to which it has gone, and it calls our affections from earth to that true life which is the great end of our being, which is the object of all our discipline, our mingled joy and suffering, here upon earth. That little child, gone from its sufferings so early, — gone

"Gentle and undefiled, with blessings on its head," —

.: has it indeed become a very angel of God for us, and is it calling us to a more spiritual life, and does it win us to heaven? Is its memory around us like a pure presence into which no thought of sin can readily enter? Or is it with us, even yet, a spiritual companion of our ways? From being the guarded and the guided, has it risen in infant innocence, yet in the knowledge and majesty of the immortal life, to be the guard and the guide? Does it, indeed, make our hearts softer and purer, and cause us to think more of duty, and live more holy, thus clothing ourselves to go and dwell with it? Does it, by its death, accomplish all this? O! most important, most glorious mission of all, if we only heed it, if we only accept it. Then shall we behold already the wisdom and benevolence of our Father breaking through the cloud that overshadows us. Already shall we see that the tie, which seemed to be dropped and broken, God has taken up to draw us closer to himself, and that it is interwoven with his all-gracious plan for our spiritual profit and perfection. And we can anticipate how it will all be reconciled, when his own hand shall wipe away our tears, and the bliss of reünion shall extract the last drop of bitterness from "the cup that our Father hath given us."

Our Relations to the Departed.

Our Relations to the Departed.

She is not dead, but sleepeth. Luke viii. 52.

A GREAT peculiarity of the Christian religion is its *transforming* or *transmuting* power. I speak not now of the regeneration which it accomplishes in the individual soul, but of the change which it works upon things without. It applies the touchstone to every fact of existence, and exposes its real value. Looking through the lens of spiritual observation, it throws the realities of life into a reverse perspective from that which is seen by the sensual eye. Objects which the world calls great it renders insignificant, and makes near and prominent things which the frivolous put far off. Thus the Christian, among other men, often appears anomalous. Often, amidst the congratulations of the world, he detects reason for mourning, and is penetrated with sorrow. On the contrary, where others shrink, he walks undaunted, and converts the scene of dread and suffering into an ante-chamber of heaven. In this light, the Apostle Paul speaks of himself and others, "As sorrowful, yet always rejoicing; as poor, yet making many rich; as having nothing, and yet possessing all things." Indeed, all the beatitudes are based upon this peculiarity; for the true blessing, the inward, everlasting riches, are for those who, in the world's eye, are poor, and mourning, and persecuted. Jesus himself weeps amid triumphant palms and sounding hosannas, while on the cross he utters the prayer of forgiveness, and the ejaculation of peace.

No wonder, then, that the believer views the ghastliest fact of all in a consoling and even a beautiful aspect; and death itself becomes but *sleep*. Well was that trait of our religion which

I have now suggested illustrated at the bed-side of Jairus' daughter. Well did that noisy, lamenting group represent the *worldly* who read only the material fact, or that flippant *scepticism* which laughs all supernatural truth to scorn. And well did Jesus represent the spirit of his doctrine, and its transforming power, when he exclaimed, "She is not dead, but sleepeth."

Yes! beautifully has Christianity transformed death. To the eye of flesh it was the final direction of our fate, — the consummate riddle in this mystery of being, — the wreck of all our hopes, —

> " The simple senses crowned his head,
> Omega ! thou art Lord, they said ;
> We find no motion in the dead."

Ever, though with higher desires and better gleamings, the mind has struggled and sunk before this fact of decay, and this awful silence of nature; while in the waning light of the soul, and among

13

the ashes of the sepulchre, scepticism has built its dreary negation. And though no mother could lay down her child without taking hints which God gave her from every little flower that sprung on that grassy bed, — though the unexhausted intellect has reasoned that we *ought* to live again, and the affections, more oracular, swelling with the nature of their great source, have prophesied that we *shall*, — never, until the revelation of Christ descended into our souls, and illuminated all our spiritual vision, have we been able to say certainly of death, it is a *sleep*. This has made its outward semblance not that of *cessation*, but of *progression* — not an *end*, but a *change* — converting its rocky couch to a birth-chamber, over-casting its shadows with beams of eternal morning, while behind its cold unconsciousness the unseen spirit broods into higher life. " He fell *asleep*," says the sacred chronicler, speaking of bloody Stephen. " Our friend Lazarus *sleepeth*," said Christ to his disciples; and yet again, as here in the text, the beautiful synonyme is repeated, "She is not dead, but sleepeth."

But I proceed to remark, if the Christian religion thus transforms death, or, in other words, abolishes the idea of its being annihilation, or an end, then it gives us a new view of *our relations to the departed.* What are these relations? The answers to this question will form the burden of the present discourse.

I. There is the relation of *memory.* It is true, we may argue that this relation exists whether the Christian view of death be correct or not; — so long have those who are now gone actually lived with us, — so vivid are their images among the realities of the soul, — though the grave should forever shut them from our communion. But this relation of memory has peculiar propriety and efficacy when associated with a Christian faith. If the dead live no more, what would memory be to us but a spectre and a sting? Should we not then seek to repress these tender recollections, --

to close our eyes to those pale, sad visions of departed love? Should we not invoke the glare and tumult of the world to distract or absorb our thoughts? Would we not say, "Let it come, the pleasure, the occupation of the hour, that we may think no more of the dead, plucked from us forever, — let us drive thoughtlessly down this swift current of life, since thought only harrows us, — let us drive thoughtlessly down, enjoying all we can, until we too lie by the side of those departed ones, like them to moulder in everlasting unconsciousness." I do not say that this would always be the case without religious hope, but it is a very natural condition of the feelings in such circumstances, — it is the most *humane* alternative that would then be left. At least, no one so well as the Christian can go into the inner chambers of memory, feel the strength of its sad yet blissful associations, and calmly invoke the communion of the dead.

I speak not now of what occurs in those first

bitter days of grief, when the heart's wound bleeds afresh at every touch, — when we are continually surprised by the bleak fact that the loved one is actually dead.   But I speak of those after seasons, those Indian summers of the soul, in which all the present desolation is blended with the bloom and enjoyment of the past.   Then do we find that the tie which binds us so tenderly to the departed is a strong and fruitful one.   We love, in those still, retired seasons, to call up the images of the dead, to let them hover around us, as real, for the hour, as any living forms.   We linger in that communion, with a pleasing melancholy.   We call up all that was lovely in their character, all that was delightful in their earthly intercourse.   They live again for us, and we for them.

In this relation of memory, moreover, we realize the fact, that while the departed were upon earth we enjoyed much with them.   This is a truth which in any estimate of our loss we should not overlook.   Do we mourn that the dead have been taken from us so soon? Are we not also thankful that they were ours so long? In our grief over unfulfilled expectation, do we cherish no gratitude for actual good? So much bliss has God mingled in our cup of existence that he might have withheld. He lent it to us thus far; why complain, rather, that he did not intrust us with it longer? O! these fond recollections, this concentrated happiness of past hours which we call up with tears, remind us that *so much good we have actually experienced.*

In close connection with this thought is the fact, that, by some delicate process of refinement, we remember of the dead only what was good. In the relation of memory we see them in their best manifestation, we live over the hours of our past intercourse. Though in extraordinary instances it may be true that "the evil which men do lives after them," yet even in regard to the illustrious dead, their imperfections are overlooked, and more justice is done to their virtues than in their own time.

Much more is this the case with those around whom our affections cling more closely. The communion of memory, far more than that of life, is unalloyed by sharp interruptions, or by any stain. That communion now, though saddened, is tender, and without reproach.

And even if we remember that while they lived our relations with them were all beautiful, shall we not believe that when they were taken away their earthly mission for us was fulfilled? Was not their departure as essential a work of the divine beneficence as their bestowal? Who knows but if they had overstayed the appointed hour, our relations with them might have changed? — some new element of discontent and unhappiness been introduced, which would have entirely altered the character of our recollections? At least, to repeat what I have just suggested, what Christian doubts that their taking away — this change from living communion to the communion of memory — was for an *end* as wise and kind as were all the love and intercourse so long vouch-safed to us?

Vital, then, for the Christian, is this relation which we have with the dead by *memory*. We linger upon it, and find in it a strange and sweet attraction. And is not much of this because, though we may be unconscious of it, the current of faith subtilely intermingles with our grief, and gives its tone to our communion? We cannot consider the departed as lost to us forever. The suggestion of *rupture* holds a latent suggestion of *reunion*. The hues of *memory* are colored by the reflection of *hope*. Religion transforms the condition of the departed for us, and we consider them not as dead, but sleeping.

II. There is another relation which we have with the dead, — the relation of *spiritual exist-ence*. We live with them, not only by communion with the past, by images of memory, but by that fine, mysterious bond which links us to all souls, and in which we live with them now and forever.

The faith that has converted death into a sleep has also transformed the whole idea of life. If the one is but a halt in the eternal march, — a slumbrous rest preceding a new morning, — the other is but the flow of one continuous stream, mated awhile with flesh, but far more intimately connected with all intelligences in the universe of God, What are the conditions of our communion with the living — those with whom we come in material contact? The eye, the lip, the hand, are but symbols, interpretations; — behind these it is only spirit that communes with spirit, even in the market or the street. But not to enter into so subtle a discussion, of what kind are some of the best communions which we have on earth? We take up some wise and virtuous book, and enter into the author's mind. Seas separate us from him, — he knows us not; he never hears our names. But have we not a close relation to him? Is there not a strong bond of spiritual communion between us? Nay, may not the intercourse we thus have with him be

better and truer than any which we could have
from actual contact, — from local acquaintance?
Then, some icy barrier of etiquette might separate
us, — some coldness of temperament upon his part,
— some spleen or disease; we might be shocked by
some temporary deformity; some little imperfection
might betray itself.   But here, in his book, which
we read three thousand miles away from him, we
receive his noblest thoughts, — his best spiritual
revelations; and we know him, and commune with
him most intimately, not through *local* but
through *spiritual* affinities.

And how pleasing is the thought that not even
death interrupts this relation.   Years, as well as
miles — ages may separate us from the great and
good man; but we hold with him still that living
communion of the spirit.   Our best life may flow
to us from this communion.   Some of our richest
spiritual treasures have been deposited in this intercourse of thought.   Some of our noblest hopes
and resolutions have been animated by those whose

lips have long since been sealed, — whose very monuments have crumbled.

A dear friend goes away from us to a foreign land. We watch the receding sail, and feel that *that* is a bond between us, until it fades away in the far blue horizon. *Then* it is a consolation to walk by the shore of that sea, and to realize that the same waters lave the other shore, where he dwells, — to watch some star, and know that at such an hour his eye and thought are also directed to it. Thus the soul will not entertain the idea of absolute separation, but makes all these material objects agents for its affinities. But how much nearer does that sbsent one come to us, when we know that at such an hour we both are kneeling in prayer, and that our spirits meet, as it were, around the footstool of God!

Thus we see that even in life there are spiritual relations which bind us to our fellows, and that often these are dearer and stronger than those of local contact. Why should we suppose that death

cuts off all such affinities? It does not cut them off.
It only removes the loved from our converse and our
sight; but if, when absent in some distant land of
this earth, we are conscious of still holding relations to them, do we not retain the same though
they have vanished into that mysterious and unseen land which lies beyond the grave? " She is
not dead, but sleepeth." Christianity has taught
us to look away from the ghastly secrets of the
sepulchre, and not consider that changing clay as
the friend we mourn, but as only the cast-off and
mouldering garment. It has kindled within us a
lively appreciation of the continued existence of
those who have gone from us; taught us to feel
that the thoughts, the love, the real life of the departed, all, in fact, that communed with us here
below, still lives and acts. And our relations to
them are the relations which we bear, not to
abstractions of memory, to phantoms of by-gone
joy, but to spiritual intelligences, whose current of
being flows on uninterrupted, with whose current

of being our own mingles. I know not how it is with others, but to me there is inexpressible consolation in this thought.

But I would suggest that, as spiritual beings, we bear even a closer relation to the departed. I said that Christianity has transformed the whole idea of life. It has shown that we are essentially spirits, and that our highest relations are spiritual. If so, it seems an arrogant assumption to deny that any intercourse may exist between ourselves and the spiritual world. Possessing as we do this mysterious nature, throbbing with the attraction of the eternal sphere, who shall say that it touches no spiritual confines, — that it has communion only with the beings that we see? It is a dull atheism which repudiates all such intimations as superstitious or absurd. To speak more distinctly, I allude to the consoling thought which springs up almost intuitively, that the departed may, at times, see us, and be present with us, though we do not recognize them. For wise and good reasons, our senses may so constrain us that we cannot perceive these spiritual beings. But the same reasons do not exist to shut them from beholding and visiting us. The most essential idea of the immortal state is that it yields certain prerogatives which we cannot possess in our mortal condition. May it not be, therefore, that while it is our lot to be restricted to sensuous vision, and to behold only material forms, it is their privilege, having received the spiritual sight, to see both spiritual and material things?

Nor need we imagine that immortality implies distance from us, — that change of state requires any great change of *place*. Looking through this earthly glass, we see but darkly; but when death shatters it we may behold close around us the friends we have loved, and find that their spiritual peculiarity is not incompatible with such near residence. The homes of departed spirits may be all around us, — those spirits themselves may be ever hovering near, unseen in our blindness of the senses. At all events, we deem it one of the grand distinctions of spirit that it is not confined to one region of space, but may pass, quick as its own intelligence, from sphere to sphere. And while I would rebuke rash speculation, I would also rebuke the cold materialism which unhesitatingly rejects an idea like this which I have now suggested.

I maintain, moreover, that such speculation is not all idle. It serves to quicken within us the thought of how *near* the dead may be to us, to purify that thought, and to breathe upon our fevered hearts a consoling hope. And when I combine its intrinsic reasonableness with the spirit and the spiritualism of Christianity, and that intuitive suggestion which springs up in so many souls, I can urge but faint objection to those who entertain it, and would, if possible, share and diffuse the comfort which it gives. Nearer, then, than we imagine — close as in mortal contact, and more intimately — may be those whom we, with earthly

vision, behold no more; visiting us in hours of
loneliness, and affording unseen companionship;
watching us in the stillness of slumber, and reflect-
ing themselves in our dreams.

But, whether we indulge this notion or not, let
us realize the relation which we have with the departed by the ties of mutual spirituality.   Let us
not coldly restrict or weaken this relation.   If the
material world is full of inexplicable things, — if
we cannot explain the secret affinities of the star
and the flower, — let us feel how full of mystery
and how full of promise is this *spiritual universe*
of which we are parts, and whose conditions we so
little know.   Let us cherish that transcendent faith,
that quick, spiritual sympathy, which says of the
departed, " They are not dead, but sleeping."

III. Finally, we have with the dead the relation
of *discipline*.   Though we should see them only
in the abstractions of memory, — though it should
be true that they have no spiritual intercourse
with us, — yet their agency in our behalf has not

ceased. They still accomplish a work for us. That work is in the moral efficacy of bereavement and sorrow. In their going away they lead our thoughts out beyond the limits of this world. They quicken us to an interest in the spiritual land. As one who looks upon a map, and listlessly reads the name of some foreign shore, so, often, do we open this blessed revelation not heeding its recital of the immortal state. But as, when some friend goes to that distant coast, that spot on the map becomes, of all places, most vivid and most prominent, so, when our loved ones die, the spiritual country largely occupies our thoughts and attracts our affections. They depart that we may be weaned from earth. They ascend that we may "look steadfastly towards heaven." If this is *not* our everlasting home, why should they all remain here to cheat us with that thought? If we *must* seek a better country, should there not be premonitions for us, breakings up, and farewells, and the hurried departure of friends who are ready before

14

us? I need not dwell upon this suggestion. We are too much of the earth earthy, and bound up in sensual interests. It is often needful that some shock of disappointment should shake our idea of terrestrial stability — should awake us to a sense of our spiritual relations — should strike open some chasm in this dead, material wall, and let in the light of the unlimited and immortal state to which we go. We need the discipline of bereavement in temporal things, to win us to things eternal. And so, in their departure, the loved accomplish for us a blessed and spiritual result, and instead of being wholly lost to us, become bound to us by a new and vital relation.

But these loved ones depart, not merely to bind our affections to another state, but to fit us better for the obligations of this. Perhaps, in the indulgence of full communion, in the liquid case of prosperity, we have scantily discharged our social duties. We have not appreciated love, because we have never felt its absence. We have shocked the ten-

derest ties, because we were ignorant of their tenderness. We have withheld good offices, because
we knew not how rare is the opportunity to fulfil
them. But when one whom we love passes away,
then, realizing a great loss, we learn how vital was
that relation, how inestimable the privilege which
is withdrawn forever. How quick then is our re-
gret for every harsh word which we have spoken
to the departed, or for any momentary alienation
which we have indulged! This, however, should
not reduce us to a morbid sensitiveness, or an
unavailing sorrow, seeing that it is blended with so
many pleasant memories; but it should teach us our
duty to the living. It should make our affections
more diligent and dutiful. It should check our
hasty words, and assuage our passions. It should
cause us, day and night, to meet in kindness and
part in peace. Our social ties are golden links of
uncertain tenure, and, one by one, they drop away.
Let us cherish a more constant love for those who
make up our family circle, for "not long may we

stay." The allotments of duty, perhaps, will soon distribute us into different spheres of action; our lines, which now fall together in a pleasant place, will be wide apart as the zones, or death will cast his shadow upon these familiar faces, and interrupt our long communion. Let us, indeed, preserve this temper with all men — those who meet us in the street, in the mart, in the most casual or selfish concerns of life. We cannot remain together a great while, at the longest. Let us meet, then, with kindness, that when we part no pang may remain. Let not a single day bear witness to the neglect or violation of any duty which we owe to our fellows. Let nothing be done which shall lie hard in the heart when it is excited to tender and solemn recollections. Let only good-will beam from faces that so soon shall be changed. Let no root of bitterness spring up in one man's bosom against another, when, ere long, nature will plant flowers upon their common grave. "Let not the sun go down upon our wrath," when his morning beams may search our accustomed places for one or both of us, in vain.

Thus, if the dead teach us to regard more dutifully the living, they will accomplish for us a most beautiful discipline.   Their departure may also serve another end.   It may teach us the great lessons of *patience* and *resignation*.   We have been surrounded by many blessings, and yet perhaps, have indulged in fretfulness.   A slight loss has irritated us.   We have chafed at ordinary disappointments, at little interruptions in the current of our prosperity.   We have been in the habit of murmuring.   And now this great grief has overtaken us, that we may see at what little things we have complained, — that we may learn that there is a meaning in trouble which should make us calm, — that we had no *right* to these gifts, the privation of which has offended us, but that all have flowed from that mercy which we have slightly acknowledged, and peevishly accused.   This great sorrow has stricken us, piercing through bone and marrow, in order to reach our hearts, and touch the springs of spiritual life within us, that henceforth we may look upon all sorrow in a new light. Little troubles have only disturbed the surface of our nature, making it uneasy, and tossing it into fretful eddies; this heavy calamity, like a mighty wind, has plunged into the very depths, and turned up the foundations, leaving us, at length, purified and serene. I believe we shall find it to be the general testimony that, those who have the least trouble are the loudest complainers; while, often, the souls that have been fairly swept and winnowed by sorrow are the most patient and Christ-like. The pressure of their woe has broken down all ordinary reliances, and driven them directly to God, where they rest in sweet submission and in calm assurance. Such is the discipline which may be wrought out for us by the departure of those we love. Such, and other spiritual results, their vanishing may secure for us, which we never could have gained by their presence; and so it may be said by some departing friend, — some one most dear to our hearts, — in a reverent sense, as the Master said to his disciples, "It is expedient for you that I go away; for if I go not away the Comforter will not come unto you."

As I have already touched upon the region of speculation, I hardly dare drop a hint which belongs here, though it grows out of a remark made under the last head. But I will say that it is not unreasonable to suppose that the departed may perform a more close and personal agency than this which I have just dwelt upon. Often, it may be, they are permitted messengers for our welfare; *guardians*, whose invisible wings shield us; *teachers*, whose unfelt instructions mysteriously sway us. The child may thus discharge an office of more than filial love for the bereaved parents. The mother may watch and minister to her child. The father, by unseen influences, win to virtue the heart of his poor prodigal. But whether this be so or not, certain are we that the departed do discharge such an agency, if not by spiritual contact with us, or direct labor in our behalf, by the chastening influence that their memory sheds upon us, by uplifting our thoughts, by spiritualizing our affections, by drawing our souls to communion with things celestial and with God.

Let us see to it, then, that we improve this discipline; that we quench not the holy aspiration which springs up in our sorrow; that we neglect not the opportunity when our hearts are softened; that we continue the prayer which first escaped our lips as a sigh and a call of distress; that the baptism of tears lets us into the new life of reconciliation, and love, and holiness. Otherwise, the discipline is of no avail, and, it may be, we harden under it.

And, finally, let me say, that the faith by which we regard our relations to the departed in the light that has been exhibited in this discourse, is a faith that must be assimilated with our entire spiritual nature. It must be illustrated in our daily conduct, and sanctify every thought and motive of our hearts. We should not seek religion merely for its consolations, and take it up as an occasional remedy. In this way religion is injured. It is associated only with sorrow, and clothed, to the eyes of men, in perpetual sadness. It is sought as the last resort, the heart's extreme unction, when it has tried the world's nostrums in vain. It is dissociated from things healthy and active, — from all ordinary experiences, — from the great whole of life. It is consigned to the darkened chamber of mourning, and the weary and disappointed spirit. Besides, to seek religion only in sorrow — to fly to it as the last refuge — argues an extreme selfishness. We have served the world and our own wills, we have lived the life of the senses, and obeyed the dictates of our passions so long as they could satisfy us, and now we turn to God because we find that he only can avail us! We seek religion for the good it can do us, not for the service we can render God. We lay hold of it selfishly, as something instituted merely for our help, and lavish our demands upon it for consolation, turning away sullen and sceptical, it may be, if these demands are not immediately answered. Many come to religion for consolation who never apply to it for instruction, for sanctification, for obedience. Let us learn that we can claim its privileges only by performing its duties. We can see with the eye of its clear, consoling faith, only when it has spiritualized our entire being, and been developed in our daily conduct. Affliction may open religious ideas in the soul, but only by the soul's discipline will those ideas expand until they become our most intimate life, and we habitually enjoy celestial companionship, and that supersensual vision of faith by which we learn our relations to the departed.

That faith let us receive and cherish. If we *live* it we shall *believe* it. No sophistry can steal it from us, no calamity make us surrender it. But the keener the trial the closer will be our confi-

dence.   Standing by that open sepulchre in which
we see our friends, " not dead, but sleeping," we
shall say to insidious scepticism and gloomy doubt,
in the earnest words of the poet,

> " O ! steal not thou my faith away,
>   Nor tempt to doubt a lowly mind.
> Make all that earth can yield thy prey,
>   But leave this heavenly gift behind.
> Our hope is but the seaboy's dream,
>   When loud winds rise in wrath and gloom ;
> Our life, a faint and fitful beam,
>   That lights us to the cold, dark tomb ;
>
> " Yet, since, as one from heaven has said,
>   There lies beyond that dreary bourn
> A region where the faithful dead
>   Eternally forget to mourn,
> Welcome the scoff, the sword, the chain,
>   The burning waste, the black abyss : —
> I shrink not from the path of pain,
>   Which leads me to that world of bliss.
>
> " Then hush, thou troubled heart ! be still ; —
>   Renounce thy vain philosophy ; —
> Seek thou to work thy Maker's will,
>   And light from heaven shall break on thee.

'T will glad thee in the weary strife,
  Where strong men sink with failing breath ;—
'T will cheer thee in the noon of life,
  And bless thee in the night of death.''

The Voices of the Dead

The Voices of the Dead.

MUCH of the communion of this earth is not by speech or actual contact, and the holiest influences fall upon us in silence. A monument or symbol shall convey a meaning which cannot be expressed; and a token of some departed one is more eloquent than words. The mere presence of a good and holy personage will move us to reverence and admiration, though he may say and do but little. So is there an *impersonal presence* of such an one; and, though far away, he converses with us, teaches and incites us. The organs of speech are only one method of the soul's expression; and the best information which it receives comes without voice or sound. We hear no vocal utterance from God, yet he speaks to us through all the forms of nature. In the blue, over-arching heaven he tells us of his comprehensive care and tender pity, and " the unwearied sun " proclaims his constant and universal benevolence. The air that wraps us close breathes of his intimate and all-pervading spirit; and the illimitable space, and the stars that sparkle abroad without number, show forth his majesty and suggest his infinitude. The gush of silent prayer — the sublimest mood of the spirit — is when we are so near to him that words cannot come between; and the power of his presence is felt the most, felt in the profoundest deep of our nature, when the curtains of his pavilion hang motionless around us. And it is so, I repeat, with all our best communions. The holiest lessons are not in the *word*, but the *life*. The virtues that attract us most are silent. The most beautiful charities go noiseless on their mission. The two mites reveal the spritual wealth beneath the poor widow's weeds; the alabaster box of ointment is fragrant with Mary's gratitude; the look of Christ rebukes Peter into penitence; and by his faith Abel, being dead, yet speaketh.

Yes, even the *dead*, long gone from us, returning no more, their places left vacant, their lineaments dimly remembered, their bodies mouldering back to dust, even these have communion with us; and to speak of "the voices of the dead" is no mere fancy. And it is to this subject that I would call your attention, in the remainder of a brief discourse.

"He being dead yet speaketh." The departed have voices for us. In order to illustrate this, I remark, in the first place, that the dead speak to us, and commune with us, *through the works which they have left behind them.* As the islands of the sea are the built-up casements of myriads of departed lives, — as the earth itself is a great catacomb, — so we who live and move upon its surface, inherit the productions and enjoy the fruits of the dead. They have bequeathed to us by far the larger portion of all that influences our thoughts, or mingles with the circumstances of our daily life. We walk through the streets they laid out. We inhabit the houses they built. We practise the customs they established. We gather wisdom from books they wrote. We pluck the ripe clusters of their experience. We boast in their achievements. And by these they speak to us. Every device and influence they have left behind tells their story, and is a voice of the dead. We feel this more impressively when we enter the customary place of one recently departed, and look around upon his work. The half-finished labor, the utensils hastily thrown aside, the material that exercised his care and received his last touch, all express him, and seem alive with his presence. By them, though dead, he speaketh to us, with a freshness and tone like his words of yesterday. How touching are those sketched forms, those unfilled outlines, in that picture which employed so fully the time and genius of the great artist — Belshazzar's feast! In the incomplete process, the transition-state of an idea from its conception to its realization, we are brought closer to the mind of the artist; we detect its springs and hid- . den workings, and therefore feel its *reality* more than in the finished effort. And this is one reason why we are more impressed at beholding the work just left than in gazing upon one that has been for a long time abandoned. Having had actual communion with the contriving mind, we recognize its presence more readily in its production; or else the recency of the departure heightens the expressiveness with which everything speaks of the departed. The dead child's cast-off garment, the toy just tossed aside, startles us as though with his renewed presence. A year hence, they will suggest him to us, but with a different effect.

But though not with such an impressive tone, yet just as much, in fact, do the productions of those long gone speak to us. Their *minds* are expressed there, and a living voice can do little more. Nay, we are admitted to a more intimate knowledge of them than was possessed by their contemporaries. The work they leave behind them is the *sum-total* of their lives — expresses their ruling passion — reveals, perhaps, their real sentiment. To the eyes of those placed on the stage with them, they walked as in a show, and each life was a narrative gradually unfolding itself. We discover the moral. We see the results of that completed history. We judge the quality and value of that life by the residuum. As "a prophet has no honor in his own country," so one may be misconceived in his own time, both to his undue disparagement, and his undue exaltation; therefore can another age better write his biography than his own. His work, his permanent result, speaks for him better — at least truer — than he spoke for himself. The rich man's wealth, — the sumptuous property, the golden pile that he has left behind him; — by it, being dead, deos he not yet speak to us? Have we not, in that gorgeous result of toiling days and anxious nights, — of brain-sweat and soul-rack, — the man himself, the cardinal purpose, the very life of his soul? which we might have surmised while he lived and wrought, but which, now that it remains the whole sum and substance of his mortal being, speaks far more emphatically than could any other voice he might have used. The expressive lineaments of the marble, the pictured canvass, the immortal poem; — by it, *Genius*, being dead, yet speaketh. To us, and not to its own time, are unhoarded the wealth of its thought and the glory of its inspiration. When it is gone, — when its lips are silent, and its heart still, — then is revealed the cherished secret over which it toiled, which was elaborated from the living alembic of the soul, through painful days and weary nights, — the sentiment which could not find expression to contemporaries, — the gift, the greatness, the lyric-power, which was disguised and unknown so long. Who, that has communed with the work of such a spirit, has not felt in every line that thrilled his soul, in every wondrous lineament that stamped itself upon his memory forever, that the dead can speak, yea, that they have voices which speak most truely, most emphatically, when they *are* dead? So does *Industry* speak, in its noble monuments, its precious fruits! So does *Maternal Affection* speak, in a chord that vibrates in the hardest heart, in the pure and better sentiment of after-years. So does *Patriotism* speak, in the soil liberated and enriched by its sufferings. So does the *martyr* speak, in the truth which triumphs by his sacrifice. So does the *great man* speak, in his life and deeds, glowing on the storied page. So does the *good man* speak, in the character and influence which he leaves behind him. The voices of the dead come to us from their works, from their results; and these are all around us.

But I remark, in the second place, that the

dead speak to us in *memory* and *association.* If
their voices may be constantly heard in their
works, we do not always heed them; neither have
we that care and attachment for the great congre-
gation of the departed which will at any time call
them up vividly before us. But in that congrega-
tion there are those whom we have known intimately and fondly, whom we cherished with our
best love, who lay close to our bosoms. And these
speak to us in a more private and peculiar manner,
— in mementos that flash upon us the whole per-
son of the departed, every physical and spiritual
lineament — in consecrated hours of recollection
that open up all the train of the past, and re-twine
its broken ties around our hearts, and make its
endearments present still. Then, then, though
dead, they speak to us. It needs not the vocal
utterance, nor the living presence, but the mood
that transforms the scene and the hour supplies
these. That face that has slept so long in the
grave, now bending upon us, pale and silent, but

affectionate still, — that more vivid recollection of every feature, tone, and movement, that brings before us the departed just as we knew them in the full flush of life and health, — that soft and consecrating spell which falls upon us, drawing in all our thoughts from the present, arresting, as it were, the current of our being, and turning it back and holding it still as the flood of actual life rushes by us,— while in that trance of soul the beings of the past are shadowed — old friends, old days, old scenes recur, familiar looks beam close upon us, familiar words reëcho in our ears, and we are closed up and absorbed with the by-gone, until tears dissolve the film from our eyes, and some shock of the actual wakes us from our reverie; — all these, I say, make the dead to commune with us as really as though in bodily form they should come out from the chambers of their mysterious silence, and speak to us. And if life consists in *experiences*, and not mere physical relations, —'and if love and communion belong to that experience, though they

take place in meditation, or dreams, or by actual
contact,—then, in that hour of remembrance, have
we really lived with the departed, and the departed
have come back and lived with us. Though dead,
they have spoken to us. And though memory
sometimes induces the spirit of heaviness,—though
it is often the agent of conscience, and wakens us
to chastise,—yet, it is wonderful how, from events
that were deeply mingled with pain, it will extract
an element of sweetness. A writer, in relating
one of the experiences of her sick-room, has illustrated this. In an hour of suffering, when no one
was near her, she went from her bed and her room
to another apartment, and looked out upon a glorious landscape of sunrise and spring-time. " I was
suffering too much to enjoy this picture at the moment," she says, " but how was it at the end of
the year ? The pains of all those hours were an-
nihilated,—as completely vanished as if they had
never been ; while the momentary peep behind the
window-curtain made me possessor of this radiant

picture for evermore." "Whence this wide difference," she asks, "between the good and the evil?
Because the good is indissolubly connected with
ideas, — with the unseen realities which are inde-
structible." And though the illustration which
she thus gives may bear the impression of an
individual peculiarity, instead of a universal truth,
still, in the instance to which I apply it, I believe
it will very generally hold true, that memory
leaves a pleasant rather than a painful impression.
At least, there is so much that is pleasant mingled
with it that we would not willingly lose the faculty of memory, — the consciousness that we can
thus call back the dead, and hear their voices, —
that we have the power of softening the rugged
realities which only suggest our loss and disappointment, by transferring the scene and the hour
to the past and the departed. And, as our conceptions become more and more spiritual, we shall
find the *real* to be less dependent upon the outward and the visible, — we shall learn how much

life there is in a thought, — how veritable are the communions of spirit; and the hour in which memory gives us the voices of the dead will be prized by us as an hour of actual experience, and such opportunities will grow more precious to us. No, we would not willingly lose this power of memory. One would not say, " Let the dead never come back to me in a thought, or a dream; let them never glide before me in the still watch of meditation; let me see, let me hear them no more, even in fancy;" — not one of us would say this; and, therefore, it is evident, that whatever painful circumstance memory or association may recall, — even though it cause us to go out and weep bitterly, — there is a sacred pleasure, a tender melancholy, that speaks to us in these voices of the dead, which we are willing to cherish and repeat. It makes our tears soft and sanctifying as they fall; it makes our hearts purer and better, — makes them stronger for the conflict of life.

I remark, finally, that the dead speak to us in

those *religious suggestions* — those consolations, invitations, and hopes —which the bereaved spirit indulges. Our meditations, concerning them naturally draw us more closely to those spiritual realities which lie beyond the grave, and beget in us those holier sentiments which we need. That such is the tendency of these recollections experience assures us. They open for us a new order of thought; they bring us in contact with the loftiest but most neglected truths. Even the hardest heart feels this influence. It is softened by the stroke of bereavement, and, for the time being, a chastening influence falls upon it, and it always thinks of the dead with tenderness and awe. They speak to our affections with an irresistible influence; they soothe our turbulent passions with their mild and holy calmness; they rebuke us in their spiritual majesty for our sensuality and our sin. They have departed, but they are not silent. Though dead, they speak to us. Sweet and sanctifying is their communion with us. They utter words of warning, too, and speak to us by the silent eloquence of example. By this they bid us imitate all that was good in their lives, all that is dear to remember. By this, too, they tell us that we are passing swiftly from the earth, and hastening to join their number. A little while ago, and they were as we are; — a little while hence, and we shall be as they. Our work, like theirs, will be left behind to speak for us. How important, then, that we consider what work we do! They assure us that nothing is perpetual here. They bid us not fasten our affections upon earth. In long procession they pass us by, with solemn voices telling of their love and hatred, their interests and cares, their work and device; — all abandoned now and passed away, as little worth as the dust that blows across their graves. Upon all that was theirs, upon every memorial of them, broods a melancholy dimness and silence. They recede more and more from the associations of the living. New tides of life roll through the cities of their habitation, and upon the foot-worn pavements of their traffic other feet are busy. Their lowly labor, or their stately pomp, is forgotten. No one weeps or cares for them. Their solicitous monuments are unheeded. The companions of their youth have rejoined them. The young, who scarcely remembered them, are giving way to another generation. The places that knew them know them no longer. " This, this," their solemn voices preach to us, " is the changeableness of earth, and the emptiness of its pursuits ! " They urge us to seek the noblest end, the unfailing treasure. They bid us find our hope and our rest, our only constant joy, in Him, who alone, amid this mutability and decay, is permanent, — in God !

Well, then, is it for us to listen to the voices of the dead. By so doing, we are better fitted for life, and for death. From that audience we go purified and strengthened into the varied discipline of our mortal state. We are willing to *stay*, knowing that the dead are so near us, and that our communion with them may be so intimate. We are willing to *go*, seeing that we shall not be wholly separated from those we leave behind. We will toil in our lot while God pleases, and when he summons us we will calmly depart. When the silver cord becomes untwined, and the golden bowl broken, — when the wheel of action stands still in the exhausted cistern of our life, — may we lie down in the light of that faith which makes so beautiful the face of the dying Christian, and has converted death's ghastly silence to a peaceful sleep; may we rise to a holier and more visible communion, in the land without a sin and without a tear; where the dead shall be closer to us than in this life; where not the partition of a shadow, or a doubt, shall come between.

Mystery and Faith.

16

Mystery and Faith.

For we walk by faith, not by sight. II CORINTHIANS v. 7.

IT needs only common experience, and but little of that, to convince us that this life is full of mystery, and at every step we take demands of us faith. For at every step we take we literally walk by faith; in every work we do we must have confidence in something which is not by sight, in something which is not yet demonstrated. Skepticism carried to its ultimate consequences is the negation of everything. It closes up the issues of all knowledge, and sunders every ligament that binds us to practical life. We must have faith in something or we stand on no premises; we can predicate nothing. It may be said that in the ex-

perience of the past we have a guide for the future;
but then, must we not have faith in experience?
Do we not trust something which is not yet demonstrated when we say, "This cause which produced
that effect yesterday will produce a similar effect
to-day or to-morrow?" How do we know — positively *know*, that it will produce that effect, and
what are the grounds of our knowledge? This
boasted "cause and effect," this "experience," what
right have we to rely upon it for one moment of the
future? Not for that moment has it demonstrated
anything; — it demonstrated for the time being,
and for the time being only; and our confidence
that it will do so again is *faith*, not sight — faith
in cause and effect, faith in experience, but faith
after all. Hume, the philosopher, has illustrated
the positions which have now been taken. "As to
past experience," says he, "it can be allowed to
give *direct* and *certain* information of those precise
objects only, and that precise period of time which
fell under its cognizance; but why this experience

should be extended to future times, and to other objects, which for aught we know may be only in appearance similar; this is the main question on which I would insist. The bread which I formerly ate nourished me; that is, a body of such sensible qualities was, at that time, endued with such secret powers; but does it follow that other bread must also nourish me at another time, and that like sensible qualities must also be attended with like secret powers? The consequence seems nowise necessary." And yet we eat our bread, day by day, without a doubt or a fear. We sow the grain and we reap the wheat, but all the work is done in faith, and the whole process is steeped in mystery. In that scattering of the golden seed, what confidence is expressed in elements that we cannot see, in beneficent agencies that we cannot control, in results that are beyond our power, and that in their growth and development are full of wonder exceeding our wisdom. Give up faith; say that we will act only upon that which is demonstrated and known, say that we will walk only so far as sight reaches, and we completely separate the present from the future, and stop all the mechanism of practical life.

But if we take a wider view of things, and consider this material universe in which we live, the great fact of mystery and the need of faith will be urged upon us by a larger and more impressive teaching. The more we learn of nature the more clearly is revealed to us this fact — that we know less than we thought we did; positively, we know more, but relatively we know less, because as we have advanced nature has stretched out into wider and wider relations. The department that was unknown to us yesterday is explored to-day. Yesterday, we thought it was all that remained to be explored, but the torch of investigation that guided us through it now flares out upon new regions we did not see before. Like one who goes with a candle into some immense cavern, presently a little circle becomes clear, the shadows vanish before him, and undefined forms grow distinct. He thinks he is

near the end, when lo! what seemed a solid boundary of rock dissolves and floats away into a depth
of darkness, the path opens into an immense void,
new shapes of mystery start out, and he learns this
much that he did not know before, that instead of
being near the end, he is only upon the threshold.
We do not mean to imply by this that we have no
positive knowledge, or that we do not increase in
knowledge. With every new discovery we positively know more and more. But the new discovery reveals the fact that more is yet to be known;
it lays open new regions, it unfolds new relations
that we had not before suspected.

We follow some tiny thread a little way, and
hold it secure, but it is connected with another
ligament, and this branches out into a third; and,
instead of exhausting the matter, we find ourselves
at the root of an infinite series, of an immense relationship, upon which we have only just opened;
and yet what we have is *positive* knowledge, is
something more added to our stock. The circle of

the *known* has positively widened, but the horizon of the *unknown* has widened also, and, instead of being to us now, as it seemed some time ago, a solid and ultimate limit, it is only an ethereal wall, only to us a relative boundary, and behind are infinite depths and mystery.   Our scientific knowledge at the present day reaches this grand result — it clears up the deception that the system of nature is mere flat, dead materiality, a few mechanical laws, a few rigid forms.   It shows that these are only the husks, the outer garments of mighty forces, of sub-tile, far-reaching agencies ; and the most common, every-day truths, that seemed stale and exhausted, become illuminated with infinite meaning, and are the blossoms of an infinite life.

The wider our circle of discovery, the wider our wonder; the more startling our conclusions, the more perplexing our questions.   We have not ex-hausted the universe; — we have just begun to see its harmony of proportion and of relations, without penetrating a fathom into its real life.   How and what is that power that works in the shooting of a crystal, and binds the obedience of a star; that shimmers in the northern Aurora, and connects by its attraction the aggregated universe; that by its unseen forces, its all-prevalent jurisdiction, holds the little compass to the north, blooms in the nebula and the flower, weaves the garment of earth and the veil of heaven, darts out in lightning, spins the calm motion of the planets, and presides mysteriously over all motion and all life?   And what *is* life, and what is death, and what a thousand things that we touch, and experience, and think we know all about?   O! as science, as nature opens upon us, we find mystery after mystery, and the demand upon the human soul is for faith, faith in high, yea, in spiritual realities; and this materialism that would shut us in to death and sense, that denies all spirit and all miracle, is shattered like a crystal sphere, and the soul rushes out into wide orbits and infinite revolutions, into life, and light, and power, that are of eternity, — that are of God!

Thus the scale is prepared for us to rise from things of sense to things of spirit, to rise from faith in nature to faith in Revelation, from the faith of La Place to the faith of Paul. No one who has studied nature aright will reject Christianity because it reveals truths that he cannot see with his naked eye, — because it speaks of things that he cannot comprehend. No one who has considered the shooting of a green blade will dogmatically deny its miracles. No one who has found in the natural world the intelligent wisdom that pervades all things, will wonder that he discovers a revelation of perfect love in Jesus Christ. "We walk by faith, not by sight," said Paul. So says every Christian; and it is of all things most rational. Faith in something higher and greater than we can see, faith in something above this narrow scene, faith in something beyond this present life, faith in realities that are not of time or sense; from all that we have now considered we claim such faith to be most rational, most natural. God, spirit, immor-

tality, instead of being inconsistent with what we
know, are what we might most legitimately deduce
from it, — what we might expect from the light
that trembles behind that curtain of mystery which
bounds all our sensuous knowledge. We do believe, the veriest skeptic believes, in something
behind that curtain of mystery; nor can he with-
hold his faith because it attaches to that which is
unseen and incomprehensible, without, as has already been shown, cutting every nerve that binds
us to practical life, and smothering every suggestion that speaks from outward nature. If he do not
believe in a God, then, or in Christ, or in immortality, let him not sneer at others because they
walk by faith and not by sight; for he also must
do so, though his faith be not in such high truths,
such spiritual realities.

The Christian's faith is in an Infinite Father and
an immortal life, and though he cannot see them,
cannot come in material contact with them, he believes them to be the greatest of realities, and he

sees them by faith, a medium as legitimate as that of sight. They are mysteries, but everything contains a mystery ; they demand of him what every day's, every hour's events demand of him — faith. Let us understand, however, that faith is not the surrendering of our minds to that which is irrational and inconsistent. These terms should not be confounded with the mysterious and the incomprehensible. That the earth moves and yet stands still is not a proposition that demands faith. It is in the province of reason to say that it cannot move and stand still at the same time. It is an inconsistency. But how the earth moves on its axis, what is that law that makes it move, is an incomprehensibility. An incomprehensibility is one thing, an inconsistency is another thing. The one conflicts with our reason, the other is beyond it. In that which conflicts with our reason we cannot have faith, but as to that which is beyond it we exercise faith every day; for we literally walk by faith and not by sight.

Who shall say, then, that God, immortality, and those high truths revealed by Jesus, are inconsistent? Do they not conform to our highest reason? Do not our deepest intuitions demand that these revelations should be true? Consult your nature, examine your own heart, consider what you are, what you want, what you feel, deeply want, keenly feel, and then say whether the Revelation of a God, a Father, and an immortal life, satisfies you as nothing else can. Take them away, and would there not be a dreary and overwhelming void? And because you have not seen God, because you have not realized immortality, because they reach beyond your present vision, because the grave shuts you in, because they are high and transcendent truths, will you reject them? Do so, and try to walk by sight alone. With that nature of yours, so full of love, with that intellect of yours so limitless in capacity, you are apparently a child of the elements, a thing of physical nature, born of the dust, and returning to it. With desires that reach out beyond the stars, with faculties that in this life just begin to bud, with affections whose bleeding tendrils cling around the departed, wrestle with death, and say to the grave, "Give up the dead! they are not thine, but mine; I feel they must be mine forever," with all these desires, capacities, affections, you walk — so far as mere sight helps you — among graves and decay, with nothing more enduring, nothing better, than three-score years and ten, the clods of the valley, the crumbling bone, and the dissolving dust! Because God and immortality are mysterious, incomprehensible, reject them, and walk only by sight? The humblest outpouring of human affection rebukes thy skepticism; the most narrow degree of human intellect prophesies beyond all this; the darkest heart, with that spark of eternal life, the yearning that moves beneath all its sensualities, and speaks for better, for more enduring things, — that rebukes thee; and in man's moral nature, in his heart and his mind, there is that which only can be satisfied, only can be explained by God and immortality. They alone, then, are rational, they alone have comprehensive vision, who walk by faith, and not by sight.

Mystery and faith, then; let what we have said concerning these be not alone for the skeptic, but for the Christian who has faith but cannot fully justify and confirm it, or who feels it faltering under some heavy burden, or who is overwhelmed by the magnitude of the truths to which it attaches, or who wishes, with a kind of half-doubt, that these things might be seen and felt. They *are* great, they are incomprehensibly great; but are they therefore untrue? Does not your heart of hearts tell you they are true? Does not that Revelation of Christ steal into your soul and feed it, satisfy it, as nothing else can, with a warm, benignant power, that makes you know its truth?

Mysteries are all about us, but faith sees light beyond and around them all. Have you recently laid down the dead in their place of rest? Cold and crushing, then, is that feeling of vacancy, that dreary sense of loss, that rushes upon you, as you look through the desolate chambers without, — through the desolate chambers of the heart within. But will not He who calls out from the very dust where yon sleepers lie the flowers of summer, and who, in the snows that enwrap their bed, cherishes the germs of the glorious springtime, will not He who works out this beautiful mystery in nature bring life from the tomb, and light out of darkness? It is truly a great mystery; but everything within us responds to it as reasonable; and though it demands our faith, who, who, in this limited and changing world, can walk by sight alone?